EVAN'S VOICE

by
Sallie Lowenstein

LION STONE BOOKS
KENSINGTON, MD

Published by
LION STONE BOOKS
4921 Aurora Drive
Kensington, Maryland 20895

Cataloging-in-Publication Data
Lowenstein, Sallie
Evan's Voice/Sallie Lowenstein
p.cm.

Summary: In a plague decimated future world, Jake must take care of his plague-stricken brother Evan after their mother abandons them. A strange storyteller who comes on television and tells tales of amazing alien worlds is the only ray of hope in this bleak world.

ISBN 0-9658486-1-2
[1. Science fiction 2. Young Adult Novel]

Library of Congress Catalog Card Number: 98-92071

First Edition
Manufactured in the United States, September 1998
Printed by Kirby Lithographic Company, Inc.

OTHER BOOKS BY
SALLIE LOWENSTEIN:
The Mt. Olympus Zoo
Daniel the Medusa Hunter
The Frame-It Alphabet Book

LIST OF ILLUSTRATIONS

****

The illustrations in the book were drawn with pen and ink on 9" X12" archival paper. No lines were used in the drawings, only dots of different densities and widths. The drawings were then reduced and scanned into the typographical frames, which were created on a computer publishing program.

"SIT UP! PAY ATTENTION!" OLD APPEL BELLOWED AT HIS CLASS THAT FIRST MORNING OF SCHOOL. "DO YOU SEE ME? MY STUDENTS CALL ME THE DINO. AND THAT'S SHORT FOR DINOSAUR. AND THAT'S JUST WHAT I AM. SO BE PREPARED BECAUSE I PROMISE, I AM GOING TO STOMP ON YOU UNTIL YOU ARE AS FLAT AS PANCAKES OR SMART ENOUGH TO GET IT."

OLD APPEL GOT FOR MR. APPEL, PRONOUNCED APPEL DEFINITELY AND IT-BIT-ATTER. THE DINO WAS LEGEND. HIS POLKA DOTTED TIE AND BUTTON DOWN SHIRT WERE LEFT

"AND JAKE, YOU AIN'T NEVER GONNA MAKE IT TO OXMOON LAND."

"MR. LAWRENCE," APPEL SAID, PRONOUNCING IT LIKE HE SAID DARPEL, WITH A LONG DASH BETWEEN SYLLABLES, "COULD YOU REPEAT THE ASSIGNMENT I JUST GAVE?" HE HEARD STIFLED SNICKERS, BUT MR. APPEL CONTINUED UNDETERRED

CHAPTER 1

The first day of school kids wandered into the class hooting and cat-calling as they saw each other. Two girls sashayed from one seat to another, puckering at the air in front of boys' faces, but Jake focused on Mr. Appel, pronounced Ap-pel, who was standing at the front of the room, absently pulling at his polka-dotted tie. He watched as Old Ap slowly raised his foot and hand at the same moment, and brought his shiny, leather shoe down with a thunderous explosion on an empty pop can.

"Heads up!" Old Ap bellowed, taking advantage of the effect as heads snapped and jaws dropped. "I'm Mr. Ap-pel, your journalism teacher, and in case you haven't heard, I'm a dinosaur left over from the 20th century." He flipped his tie for emphasis and pulled at his button-down collar. "And, because I was born so long ago and am such a dinosaur, almost fossilized in fact, I expect you to work in this class. If you don't meet my standards, I will stomp you as flat as this can under my foot. Got it?"

The Dino, as all the kids called him, definitely had everyone's attention. It was silent in the room. Jake shrank low into his seat and prayed the crazy, old dinosaur didn't notice him. The only thing he was hoping for this year was a little notice from girls. That made his friends laugh.

"What girl is gonna look at you, Jake? Girls just wanna get to Gizmo-land and you know why. 'Gizmos don't got to labor, got to worry, got to think, cause machines do it all in Gizmo-land'," his friends said, chanting a popular saying. "And Jake, you ain't never gonna make it to Gizmo-land, that's for sure and true."

"Mr. Law-rence," Ap said, pronouncing it like he said Ap-pel with a long dash between syllables, "could you repeat the assignment I just gave?"

"Huh? Uh, I was thinking," he grasped desperately for an excuse, "and didn't hear you."

"Thinking? About what? I'm curious."

"Uh, I dunno," he stammered and heard high-pitched girl laughs.

"And you also don't know what the assignment is?"

"No, sir."

"How do you intend to do it?"

"I dunno that either."

"So you want to be my first 'stompee' of the year?"

"Okay," he said, "sure."

He heard stifled snickers, but Mr. Ap-pel continued undeterred. "Mr. Law-rence, since this is a journalism class, I think it would be most appropriate to have you identify a famous, living individual whom you think would be interesting to interview."

"That's it?" He had expected worse.

"And then tell me why in fifteen-hundred words. You've got two days," the Dino said threateningly.

The bell buzzed and the class quickly gathered books, jackets, lunches and bolted into the hall. Mr. Jake Lawrence was the first one out the door.

By lunch he was starving. From his corner of the cafeteria he scoped out the room. Nervous nibblers lined up along the walls and gobbled their lunches. Highbrow girls smugly occupied a side table and ignored everyone else. The Junior Tattoos sauntered in, taking care that a prettied-up group of girls took note of them before leisurely sitting at their regular table. Jake had to try hard not to look at them so he wouldn't laugh. Some day they might be like their fathers and uncles and brothers who roamed the streets in packs like jackals, but for now, they just looked silly strutting their airs. He knew he could take a Junior Tattoo with his eyes closed. One-on-one he could take just about anybody, even an adult, but he'd be real dumb to provoke a gang. He clamped his lips into a straight line as the drumming of fists against tabletops to mark out territories heightened, and the screams of anger and conversation rose into a howl, and all his thoughts drowned in the noise and fury.

"Hey, Jake," Arty Leroy said right into his ear as he joined him. "Who you gonna pick to interview, huh?"

"Uh, I ain't decided in the last couple hours. Got any suggestions?"

"Make it good, or the Dino's gonna stomp you."

"Duh," Jake said.

"Did ya see there's gonna be a new wee-hour, 2D video show on tomorrow morning?" Arty asked.

"So, they got another wonderful offering for us again, huh?" Jake said sarcastically.

"It's better than zip, but I gotta work for Pops Macarni at his web-site before school, so I ain't gonna getta watch. You gonna watch?"

"How long you working for, Arty?"

"Got lucky, got two mornings this time. You gonna watch the show, yes or no?"

"Sure, why not?"

"Let me know whatcha think of it, okay?"

"You ain't expecting much, are you?"

"Course not! I'd hafta be stupid to do that."

The buzzer went off. Lunch ended and he had missed all the action talking to Arty about a wee-hours show that wasn't even going to be worth watching. Free 2DV just filled the stations' public service obligations. All the good stuff was on 3DV, and the Gizmos kept that for themselves. Once when someone bombed open a DV store, Jake had jumped into a Three Dimensional Vision Broadcast and felt it all, all of it! The smells, the excitement, the textures. All of it! Two DV was a joke.

He got up and sauntered out, making sure his orange and brown skin-tights were pulled straight. Even if he

hadn't caught a girl looking at him when he wore them, and even if they were only charity hand-me-downs from one of Ma's boyfriends, they were pretty cool duds. Too bad he couldn't wear them every day.

"Hey, Jake," Mellie called. Guess she was a girl, but she dressed almost as bad as Mr. Ap-pel. Her hair was curled into tight, black wads, and she didn't wear make-up and her ears stuck out too much.

"Hi," he said anyway, cause at least she was nice.

"Heard you didn't get off to such a good start with Mr. Appel today."

"Yeah, well if you call him 'Apple' like that to his face, instead of Ap-pel, he'll get you, too," Jake said, trying not to stare at the huge earrings she was wearing as they swung like pendulums from her big ears.

"I know. Wanna study together later?"

"Maybe another time, Mellie. I can't today."

What he wanted was to cut Evol and Genetics, but he was determined he would develop a better reputation at school and make better choices this year. So, he went to the class, but for all the attention he paid to gene mapping, he might as well have cut. Thinking about Ma had made him think about that big-shot Alen Daymint, Ma's boyfriend of the moment. The way Alen used his ma made Jake mad. When it was convenient, Alen just oozed the charm, and Ma fell for it, over and over, making bad choices, until he and Evan hardly ever saw her.

Long after all the kids had scattered, he sat on the wet ground under the lone schoolyard tree. He stared at his long fingers and bony knees and knew why no girl looked at him. He was too skinny. Ma used to tell him his eyes were Periwinkle, but he had always known they were just watery blue, and that his teeth were too big for his jaw. If he'd been a rich Gizmo kid, his teeth would have been straightened already. He yanked his pants legs down on his extra long legs that just kept getting longer and longer, got up and walked home to Evan.

"You're late," Ma yelled. "How many times I got to tell you to come home on time? I got to work!" She slammed out of the door.

Evan was seven and still couldn't talk. Ma said it was the Plague. Evan had been born long after its height, but Ma still claimed it was the Plague that had marked him. Evan was seven and Ma said he was dumb as a doorknob, but it didn't matter to Jake, because Evan and Jake loved each other. Jake read to Evan every night. He read him first readers, he read him comic books, he read him his Evol book. Jake hoped if he said each word crisply Evan might talk or repeat a sound. He didn't, but Jake kept it up. He needed a brother to tell secrets to, to climb trees with, to tell jokes and stories to, and even though Evan couldn't do anything like that, he could hug Jake. Jake took what he could get and they often fell asleep together on the sofa until Ma came home at 5:30 in the morning, like she did most mornings, and made them get up and start over.

This morning, the old lady from across the hall knocked on the door.

"Jake, oh Jake, up and at 'em. Your ma called and asked me to watch Evan today. Come on, up, up. It's already 5:40," Mrs. Garvey called into the apartment.

He rubbed his eyes and splashed icy water on them to wake up. It was dark out still, but the apartment was cast with light from the windows that echoed around the room defining furniture and ceiling, floor and sleeping child. He kissed Evan, whose beautiful brown eyes fluttered open, startled and wary.

"It's okay, little man. Come on, let's eat. Oh drat, I gotta watch a show for a friend first. Wanna watch?"

He gathered Evan and swaddled him in blankets on the sofa.

EVAN WAS SEVEN AND STILL COULDN'T TALK. MA SAID IT WAS THE PLAGUE. EVAN HAD BEEN BORN LONG AFTER ITS HEIGHT, BUT MA STILL CLAIMED IT WAS THE PLAGUE THAT HAD MARKED HIM. EVAN WAS SEVEN AND MA SAID HE WAS DUMB AS A DOORKNOB, BUT IT DIDN'T MATTER TO JAKE, BECAUSE EVAN LOVED HIM. JAKE READ TO HIM EVERY NIGHT. HE READ HIM FIRST READERS, HE READ HIM COMIC BOOKS, HE READ HIM HIS EVO BOOK. JAKE HOPED IF HE SAID EACH WORD CRISPLY EVAN MIGHT TALK OR REPEAT A SOUND. HE DIDN'T, BUT JAKE KEPT IT UP. HE NEEDED A BROTHER TO TELL SECRETS TO, TO CLIMB TREES WITH, TO TELL JOKES AND STORIES TO, AND EVEN THOUGH EVAN COULDN'T DO ANYTHING LIKE THAT, HE COULD HUG JAKE. JAKE TOOK WHAT HE COULD GET AND THEY OFTEN FELL ASLEEP TOGETHER ON THE SOFA UNTIL MA CAME HOME AT 5:30 IN THE MORNING LIKE SHE DID MOST MORNINGS, AND MADE THEM GET UP AND START OVER.

HE KISSED EVAN WHOSE BEAUTIFUL BROWN EYES FLUTTERED OPEN, STARTLED AND WARY.

"IT'S OKAY, LITTLE MAN. COME ON, LET'S EAT. OH DRAT! I GOTTA WATCH A SHOW FOR A FRIEND

FIRST. WANNA WATCH?"

HE GATHERED EVAN AND SWADDLED HIM IN BLANKETS ON THE SOFA. "NOW IT

MIGHT BE GOOD, YOU NEVER CAN TELL. LET'S SEE WHAT WE GOT HERE."

HE FLICKED THE DIAL AND SETTLED BACK ON THE COUCH. THE ADS WERE ON AND JAKE

LET HIS MIND WANDER TO HIS FAVORITE DREAM. EVAN HAD A TUTOR AL AND EVAN WAS E A NURSE

WHILE HE HAD ACCESS TO SCHOOL FROM HOME. LIFE THERE HAD ... WAS DID NO MORE LUNATICS LEFT OUR FROM

"Now it might be good, you never can tell. Let's see what we got here."

He flicked the dial and settled back on the couch. The ads were on and Jake let his mind wander to his favorite dream. Evan had a tutorial and maybe a nurse, while he had access to school from home like the richy Gizmos did. No more lunatics left over from another century trying to teach anybody anything they could. No more laboriously writing papers by hand because he couldn't afford basic gizmo-tech.

"You up Jake?" Mrs. Garvey called. "You decent so I can come in and help you guys?"

"Sure, sure, Mrs. Garvey," he called back as he pulled on his pants.

"Now," the old lady said, coming in the door. "I keep telling your ma to lock the door and she keeps saying, 'Why? There's nothing to steal,' and I keep saying, 'They could steal your kids,' and she says back, 'Why?' But I think a lot of people would pay for you two," she said softly.

"Yeah, yeah, sure, sure. A lot you know about kids, Mrs. Garvey," Jake said. "Nobody'd want us."

"I know beautiful children when I see them, Jake. A lot of people would have paid for a baby that looked like you. That coffee and cream skin, set off by those pearly-blue eyes. Those eyes will be your ticket some day."

He kissed the old lady on the cheek. "I'll take you with me when I go, Mrs. Garvey."

"Those eyes and that sweet nature," she said.

If she saw him on the street she wouldn't think that. Out on the streets those pearly blues narrowed into cagey, black slits.

She toddled off to the kitchen and Jake curled himself around Evan as the show finally came on. An old man sat in empty space, his eyes glowing a bit. For 2DV the special effects didn't seem bad, at least until they blared the announcement of the sponsor's name out over the music which had been softly, pleasantly rising to fill the void.

"Leave it to Arty to get me to watch something this lame, eh Evan?"

There was an awkward moment as the old man's face shifted in and out of focus, and atonal music flared up loudly. The old man scowled.

"Now this is really bad, ain't it Evan?"

The music cut off in the middle of a note and there was another blank pause.

"I'd be snarling if I had a tech crew like the one producing this show," he told Evan.

The old man began at last. His voice was surprisingly melodious, and Jake, who had been about to turn off the DV, sat back down.

"Well, his voice is nice anyways," he said to his silent brother as the rhythm of the words began to weave its spell.

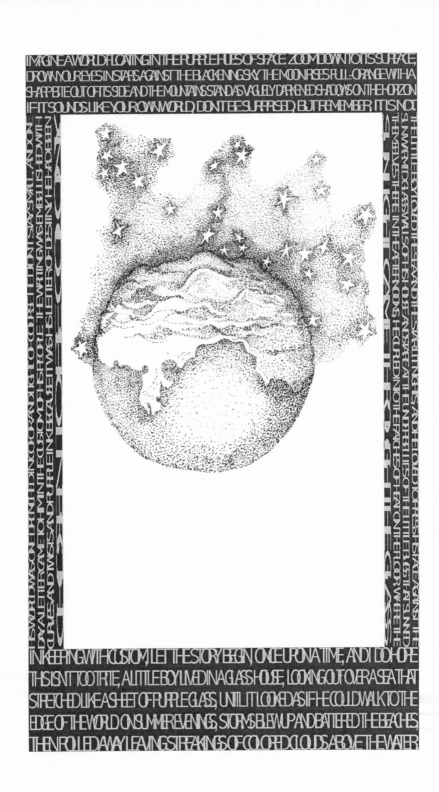

CHAPTER 2

Imagine a world floating in the purple hues of space. Zoom down to its surface, drown your eyes in stars against the blackening sky. The moon rises full-orange with a sharp bite out of its side and the mountains stand as vaguely, darkened shadows on the horizon.

If it sounds like your own world, don't be surprised, but remember it is not.

In keeping with custom, let the story begin, once upon a time, and I do hope this isn't too trite, a little boy lived in a crystal house, looking out over a sea that stretched and stretched like a sheet of purple glass, until it looked as if he could walk to the edge of the world. On summer evenings, storms blew up and battered the beaches, then rolled away leaving streakings of colored clouds above the water.

The little boy loved the sea and the starlit nights, and he loved to press his face against the sun-warmed glass walls of his house and stare at the underbellies of the little bugs that sunned themselves there. In the afternoons, he curled into patches of heat on the floor, where the sunlight came through the glass. His world was one drenched in color and light. Of course he didn't stay small, and one day a letter came to him in the custom of his people. The writing was embellished with curves, and twists, and purple ink because it was his letter of destiny. He had been chosen for Colony.

His Colony was to gather in one year to begin their great trip. His mother cried and his father ranted, "This isn't fair, it simply isn't fair. We have only one child."

His parents wrote long letters of complaint, but it did no good. When the boy was ten, they packed his clothes and favorite books, his soft animals and his bug collecting kit, his stick ball and his flute, and took him to Colony. They kissed him and hugged him and tore themselves from him as he joined his new family, his Colony. Within a week they were in the deep, cold maws of space, without any warm spots in which to nap.

A burping microphone broke the rhythm of the story and a throaty-voice said, "Aw, doggonit. Well, time's up anyway."

The old man opened his mouth to protest, but his sound had been cut off.

"Those idiots! I wanted to know what happened, didn't you, Evan?" Jake said, even as the screen went black. "Geez, whata way to end a story. Course, we don't never expect much from Gizmos, do we?"

"You've got to go to school anyway, Jake," Mrs. Garvey said. "Maybe they'll finish the story tomorrow."

Oh, sure, Jake thought. All they ever do is tantalize us and then cut our rope. Same old, same old. What is "colony" anyway?

He pulled on his shoes, noticing a second hole in the toe that matched the one in the sole. Didn't matter, he didn't have money for new ones.

He combed his fingers through his curls, but they still popped up, soft, reddish brown and annoying. "Girl's hair," the boys teased him.

"Hey now, Evan," he said as he bent down to kiss the child, "Mrs. Garvey'll take care of everything til Ma comes."

He saw a small glint in the silent eyes and squeezed the flaccid little hands.

"It'll be a good day." He kissed his brother and started for the door.

"Slow there, Jake. Here's your lunch." Mrs. Garvey thrust the bag into his hands. "And don't you go hanging with those good-for-nothings down on the street."

The old lady was pretty okay, maybe a bit twentieth, but okay.

The minute he set foot on the sidewalk, his eyes darted side and about, and his fingers itched near his knife. He kept his knife sparkling and glint-edged. If blood got on the blade today, he'd be able to clean it quickly in gutter water from last night's rain. He never took his knife back to the apartment bloody. The blood stayed in the street, away from Evan.

He stepped up his walking pace. School was a considerable walk unless he cut corners and went diagonally, but that could get him boxed in by somebody a long way from nowhere. He stuck to the walkways.

When he looked up he couldn't see the sky, only the piping and cross bars. The sky in Jake's part of town was kaput, blocked out, gone. Sky for the kid in the story had vanished, too. No sky for either of them, but at least the Colony kid had seen open sky and the ocean. Jake ached for that vastness of which the old man had spoken.

He stopped a few blocks from school and looked up again. Years ago he had found that if he squinted and put up his hands to block out the surroundings at this particular spot, he could glimpse a small sliver of sky.

A bell rang in the distance. Late again. He readied himself as he hurried towards the gates.

"Well, if it ain't Late-Jake," Alvin the guard winked. "Why do you keep coming, kid? I can never figure it. Hurry up, hurry up. Don't your mother tell you to get here quick?"

"Yeah, yeah."

"Well, you're gonna be too late one day, you know. Then whatcha gonna do?"

Jake ducked past Alvin and ran across the school yard, slipped in just as the gates slammed and the school doors locked tightly behind him. Some kids said real-time school was jail for everyone they didn't have juvey space for. Maybe that was what Colony was, juvey time.

By the time he got to Mr. Ap-pel's class he was tired. He put his head down, just to close his eyes for a second and when he opened them, Ap-pel was standing over him and the class was gone.

"Are you sick, Mr. Law-rence?" he asked.

HE STEPPED UP HIS WALKING PACE SCHOOL WAS A LONG WAY UNLESS HE CUT THE CORNERS AND WENT DIAGONALLY BUT THAT COULD GET HIM BOXED IN BY SOMEBODY A LONG WAY FROM ANYWHERE HE STUCK TO THE WALKS WHEN HE LOOKED UP HE COULDN'T SEE THE SKY ONLY THE RAILING AND CROSS BARS IN THIS PART OF TOWN THE SKY IN JAKE'S PART OF TOWN WAS KAPUT BLOTTED OUT GONE SKY FOR THE KID IN THE STORM HAD VANISHED TOO

"Uh, no, just tired, I guess."

"So I see, but I would point out to you that tired, inattentive people tend to become the unsuspecting prey of aroused dinosaurs, and you, Mr. Law-rence have aroused me. In order to soothe my ferocious temperament, you will provide me with a more extensive report on the famous person you are writing about. It will now include an interview with that person which will be due in a few weeks. You haven't forgotten that yesterday's assignment is due tomorrow, have you?"

"I ain't forgotten, but Mr. Ap-pel, how am I gonna get an interview with someone famous?" Jake protested.

"It's 'going to get', and that is not my problem."

"But ..."

"But, you should have been paying attention! Now hurry, or you'll be in hot water with your next teacher as well."

He hurried along, but the next class faded into the background as he worried over whom he was going to choose to write about for Ap. He couldn't just pick up and go to the library to research the problem. He had Evan at home, and no library credit because his ma would never co-sign with him. And, it wasn't like a Streetie kid knew anybody famous to begin with.

"Hey, Jake," Arty said at lunch, "how was the show?"

"Huh? Oh, I liked it. So did Evan."

"Evan? Right, like Evan likes anything."

"Hey, Arty, I don't take nothing about Evan from no one, get it?" Jake said as he felt his cheeks and ears begin to burn.

"Sure, sure, Jake. Sorry, really."

"Yeah," Jake said, gathered his lunch and went to sit at another table. Arty was a pain. Anyone else said anything about Evan today, he'd knock their heads off.

He doodled through the last class. When he looked down, he realized he'd drawn lots of little yellow bugs. Maybe Alvin was right, maybe he should quit school, just not come back. Ma would never know. She was never home. Who would care?

"Mr. Law-rence?" Mr. Ap-pel was waiting for him outside the school. "I am going to the library. I wondered if you would like to accompany me?"

"Uh, I don't got no library credit, and I gotta go home to take care of my brother, so thanks, but no thanks."

He started walking fast and was surprised to find the old man keeping pace with him.

"Well then, you are in a bind, as I assume you do not have an interviewee in mind."

Jake sliced away from Old Ap and kept walking until he passed out the school gates and back onto the street. He nibbled the remains of his lunch sandwich, and pondered what he was going to do about the assignment, but not for long. Instead, the image of a purple earth, its surface tickled by gentle air currents and dappled by the blue-grey shadows of clouds, filled his mind.

He craved the rest of the story. If they didn't put the show back on, he'd ask the DV station who the storyteller was. If the station wouldn't tell a kid from a lock-in-school, he'd wait outside the studio until the old man came out. He was going to hear the rest of that story!

He absently kicked at broken concrete. The sound of a little chunk cracking off snapped his head up. Daydreaming didn't keep you alive long on the street. It was like baiting the jackals, daydreaming was. It could end in bloodletting. He didn't like drawing blood, but he liked getting nicked even less. He rubbed his hand on the hilt of his knife, kicking at a bit of concrete the rest of the way home as a reminder to stay alert.

JAKE SLICED AWAY IN ANOTHER DIRECTION AND KEPT WALKING UNTIL HE PASSED
OUT THE SCHOOL GATES AND BACK ONTO THE STREETS. HE NIBBLED THE REMAINS OF HIS
MOIST SANDWICH AND PONDERED WHAT HE WAS GOING TO DO ABOUT THE ASTON MIN...

HE ABSENTLY KICKED AT BROKEN CONCRETE. THE SOUND OF A LITTLE CHUNK CRACKING OFF SNAPPED
HIS HEAD UP. DAYDREAMING COULDN'T KEEP YOU ALIVE ON THE STREET. IT WAS LIKE BATTING THE JACK. AS DAY-
DREAMING WAS, IT COULD END IN BLOOD LETTING. HE DIDN'T LIKE DRAWING BLOOD, DID HE, BUT HE LIKED GETTING
NICKED EVEN LESS. HE FEED HIS HAND ON THE JUT OF THE KNIFE, KICKING THE BIT OF CONCRETE THE FIRST OF
THE EXXXAML TO ME AS A REMINDER TO STAY ALERT.

"So there you are at last, Jake," his ma said. "I keep telling you, I need you home on time! I hope you pay better attention in school than you do to me."

His ma was pretty, real pretty. All his friends told him how pretty she was. Truth was he hated it. The few pennies she earned went into making her pretty. All her nights were filled up because of being pretty. Her hair used to be long and silky, and he could remember how she had smelled so good after a shampoo, and how the room had smelled of her. After she got pretty, she cut her hair to be like all the rich Gizmo women. She went to school, too, just long enough to learn how to speak rich. He wished she was just Ma, not Pretty Ma.

"I pay about as much attention in school as you pay to me and Evan, Ma," he said back to her.

"I warned you, you better do good, or I'm not taking you with me when I leave this hole. Do you think I'm kidding, Jake?"

"Yeah, Ma, kidding yourself if you think any of your boyfriends are gonna take you offa the street. Face it, you're stuck in this dump with me and Evan forever." He knew he shouldn't have said it as soon as it slipped out.

She turned on him, jamming her face right up in his, her lips trembling. "Watch your mouth or you're gonna be real sorry!"

"Why should I? You don't care about Evan and me. You ain't even here no more. Mrs. Garvey feeds us and kicks me out more mornings than you do!" he said, his anger taking on a voice of its own.

"That cuts it. Now, I'm not taking you with me!"

"Don't matter. I wasn't going without Evan anyways, and you wasn't taking him, was you, Ma? Your men don't even know about Evan, do they, Ma? Were you gonna help Evan, too? Were you, Ma?"

"Just shut your mouth! I can't do anything for Evan."

"Why should I shut my mouth, Ma? So you can pretend you ain't doing nothing wrong? You gonna take me with you and just leave Evan here? Give me a break, Ma."

A dark line appeared between her eyes and her mouth twisted. She wasn't pretty now.

"If I've told you once, I've told you twice and three times and twenty times. I'm warning you, don't push me about Evan," she snarled. "I don't owe him or you nothing," she said, her grammar slipping back to street talk. "I'm fed up to here with you and your stupid little brother. You think I wanna come home to you and Evan? You think I wanna piss away my hard-earned money on food for you two slimes? I ain't gotta stay here no more. I'm finally gonna live some place better than this rat trap!"

"Yeah, Ma, with some man? Which one this time?"

"You two ain't gonna drag me down no more!" She was yelling now, her voice rising shrilly. "You ain't gonna amount to nothing anyways, even if I stay. No more disrespect from no snot-nosed teenage kid! This time I got a guy who'll keep me nice. I'm outta here and you ain't gonna have nobody to blame but you when you're sitting here starving in this dump," she finished triumphantly.

"Go then, go on! Finish it at last," he screamed back, feeling his stomach lurch.

"I will!"

She did. She left. Threw a few fancy clothes and all her shampoos and her cheap perfumes in a case, and left. Behind her, the silence was very cold. Jake shivered.

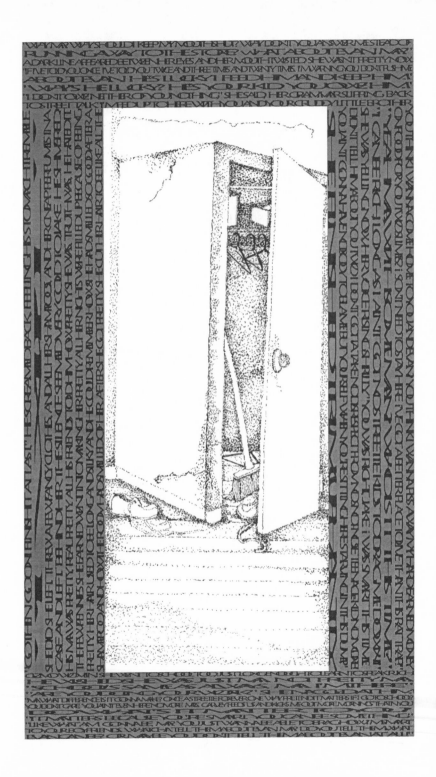

CHAPTER 3

Mrs. Garvey must have heard it all because a little while later she tapped lightly on the door.

"What happened, Jake?" she asked.

"Ma left. Packed some stuff and slammed outta here."

"Oh my, oh my," Mrs. Garvey said. "Well, I bet she comes back."

"Maybe she will and maybe she won't. It don't matter. I'll work."

"Jake, you'd have to quit school! You're too smart to drop out. About the only thing your ma and I ever agreed on was how smart you are."

"Oh yeah?" He almost laughed.

"Look Jake, I could use some company. Why don't you and Evan move in with me?"

"But, if Ma comes back she'll want the apartment."

"At least think about it. I don't think you're ready to be on your own, especially with Evan as a responsibility."

She patted his shoulder and hugged Evan. Funny, he'd never been in Mrs. Garvey's apartment, and here she was inviting them in to stay with her. He went into the kitchen. Not much to eat there, a few eggs and some onions. He'd fry them up and feed Evan.

Evan was a good eater. He liked everything, even if he did drool a little, and even if he ate with his fingers. All it meant was cleaning up after him a little more. Ma hated how Evan ate, had been embarrassed by Evan all the time. It didn't bother Jake.

He looked through the cupboards some more. What food there was wouldn't last long. He dumped the onions in a pan and they got thin and white. He cracked the eggs and pulled them apart without dropping even a tiny shell-bit into the pan. Maybe he could get a job as a cook

somewhere. School wasn't so important. No matter how much school he had, he'd never be a Gizmo.

Mrs. Garvey knocked again as they finished eating.

"How about some dessert, boys?" She had slices of warm cake covered in little red fruits on glass plates. "I thought you could use some comfort food, seeing as how your ma is gone."

"Mrs. Garvey, if you've got the dough to buy fruit and sugar, how come you live in a dump like this?" Jake asked, savoring the sweetness as he ate, while Evan put a finger through a fruit and sucked on it.

She laughed. "I lived here before it was a 'dump.' Did you fellows know this building used to have flower gardens all around it, and a fancy doorman in a shiny uniform downstairs on the stoop?"

"Yeah? What happened?" Jake asked sarcastically.

"Neighborhoods change, that's all, Jake," she said looking away from him.

He was instantly sorry he'd spoken like that to Mrs. Garvey. Mrs. Garvey was the only person who treated Evan with any respect. She was always nice to them, always there, even when their ma wasn't. He should talk nicely to her. She deserved it.

"I'm sorry, Mrs. Garvey. Maybe Evan and me could come over tonight, maybe, seeing as how Ma is gone."

"Of course you can, Jake, but if you live with me you have to go to school. I'm not looking after Evan so you can get yourself into trouble on the streets."

"Okay then, Mrs. Garvey, for a while, at least, and thanks." He paused. "Do you think she's gone for good, Mrs. Garvey?"

"I don't know, Jake. I wish I did."

"Yeah," he said. "Me too."

Not that his Ma hadn't been gone most of the time

since she had cut her hair, but if she was gone for good, it was different.

"We'll be over in a little while, Mrs. Garvey."

"Don't be long. I think that new DV show you liked is coming on again soon. It might be on a little too late for Evan, but I suppose he can sleep in tomorrow morning."

"Okay, we'll hurry. See you in a few minutes."

He gathered his books and a few clothes for each of them, and dumped them into a garbage bag.

"Come on, Evan," he said, guiding him with his hands to the door.

Evan stopped and wouldn't move.

"Come on, Evan. I'm coming too. It's just across the hall. Oh shoot," he said as he picked up the younger boy, who began to heave in dry, soundless sobs.

"Mrs. Garvey," he called loudly, "could you open up?"

The old lady opened the door and he waddled in with the now-struggling Evan.

"He's never been in anyone else's place before. The only times he leaves our place is when I take him for a walk," Jake explained. "I think he knows something happened."

"Poor thing," Mrs. Garvey whispered, stroking the child's forehead.

Mrs. Garvey's place sure was a surprise. The rooms were spacious and many, not just two cubbyholes with a kitchen and a grimy bathroom behind a screen. Tall rows of windows filled the outside walls of her apartment, and if he peered past the girders and pipes, he could make out sky sprinkled with stars. The furniture was wooden, the beds filled by soft mattresses that curled around Evan like enfolding arms when he fell asleep. Mrs. Garvey wasn't poor like them. Jake had never seen things like she had.

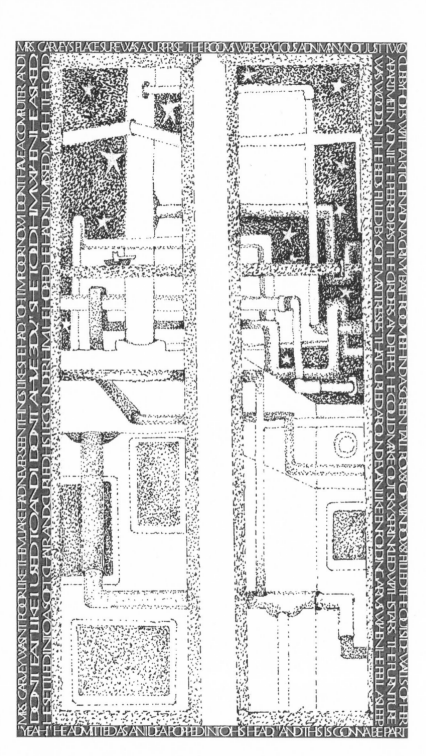

MRS. CARVEY'S PLACE SURE WAS A SURPRISE. THE ROOMS WERE SPACIOUS, AND MANY, NOT JUST TWO

YEAH, HE ADMITTED AS AN IDEA POPPED INTO HIS HEAD. AND THIS IS GONNA BE PART

"Oh, I'm poor now. I don't have a computer, and I don't eat like I used to, and I don't have 3DV," she told him when he asked.

"Mrs. Garvey, the show! What time's it supposed to be on?"

"My goodness, it's already on, but don't you have homework, Jake?"

"Yeah," he admitted as an idea popped into his head, "and this is gonna be part of it. This storyteller is on DV, so he must be famous, right?"

"Well, perhaps a little famous, Jake."

"That's good enough! Watching is gonna be part of a school project I gotta do."

He settled into a soft chair and curled his legs under him. He hoped he hadn't missed much. The old man was already speaking.

The boy, whose name was Acob Dam, quickly learned where the best ports were to watch the stars. They were cold light, but at least they sparkled. And he made a friend, a girl about his age, named Timiial. She had a pale fuzz of hair that curled around her ears, and thin bones like those of some delicate flying thing. What he liked best was the sunshine that her voice brought to him. He craved sunshine greatly.

Timiial and he spent hours together in the Colony library, faces pressed against screens, scanning what kinds of life forms they might like to live among.

"They all look so strange, so unnatural," Timiial said one day. "I don't think I want to be any of them."

"Then, let's just stay us, you and me, Timiial and Acob," he suggested.

"You know we can't, but let's promise we'll stay together."

They were twelve the day they made the pledge and had not yet begun Colony classes, did not yet know the rules.

THE BOY WHO GREW UP WAS A GOOD MAN, QUICKLY LEARNED WHERE THE BEST FORTUNES WERE, OUT AMONG THE STARS
THEY WERE COLD LIGHT, BUT AT LEAST THEY SPARKED AND HE MADE A FRIEND, A GIRL ABOUT HIS AGE NAMED
TIMIA, SHE HAD A FALL OF FUZZ OF HAIR THAT CURLED AROUND HER EARS AND THIN BONES LIKE THOSE OF SOME
DELICATE FLYING THING. WHAT HE LIKED BEST WAS THE SUNSHINE IN HER VOICE, BROUGHT TO HIM HE CRAVED

SUNSHINE AGAIN

TIMIA AND HE SPENT HOURS TOGETHER IN THE COLONY LIBRARY, FACES PRESSED AGAINST
SCREENS, SCANNING WHAT KIND OF LIFE FORMS THEY MIGHT LIKE TO LIVE AMONG

"THEY'LL LOOK SO STRANGE, SO UNNATURAL," TIMIA SAID ONE DAY, "I DON'T THINK I WANT TO BE ANY OF THEM."
"THEN LET'S JUST STAY US, YOU AND ME, TIMIA, AND JACOBS," HE HAD SUGGESTED.
"YOU KNOW WE CAN'T. BUT LET'S PROMISE WE'LL STAY TOGETHER."
THEY WERE TWELVE THE DAY THEY MADE THEIR PLEDGE, AND HAD NO YET BEGUN COLONY

CLASSES DID NOT YET KNOW THE RULES

THE LIGHT SCRAWLED UPON THE OLD MAN'S FACE AND FOR AN INSTANT HE LOOKED YOUNG TO JAKE
THEN HE GROWLED AT SOMEONE OFF CAMERA. "I'M NOT YET FINISHED," THE OLD MAN INSISTED
"YEAH, YOU ARE. THAT'S IT FOR TONIGHT. TIME'S UP NOW, VAMOOSE." A VOICE SAID

VAMOOSE, VANISH!" THE STORYTELLER ASKED

"I WOULD BE HAPPY TO OBLIGE."
AND HE DID. HE VANISHED. IT WAS A GREAT ENDING, A REALLY GOOD GAG
MRS. GALVEZ AND JAKE SMILED AT EACH OTHER

The lights came up on the old man's face and for an instant he looked young to Jake.

"I'm not yet finished," the old man growled at someone off camera.

"Yeah, you are. That's it for tonight. Time's up. Now vamoose," a voice said.

"Vamoose, vanish?" the storyteller asked.

"Yeah."

"I would be happy to oblige."

And he did. He vanished. It was a great ending, a really good gag. Mrs. Garvey and Jake smiled at each other.

"Now that was refreshing," Mrs. Garvey said.

"Except that I missed most of it. Is it on again in the morning?"

"I think so."

"Good. I'm gonna write him up now. What's the old man's name?"

"I don't know, sweetie. Why?"

"Cause I gotta know to write my report. Guess I'll just hafta call him the Storyteller."

"Why don't you dial up the DV station and ask?"

"Mrs. Garvey, we don't got a phone."

"No, but I do and I have lots of credit built up."

He should have known Mrs. Garvey had a phone because his ma was always calling her to ask her to look in on him and Evan.

"I can't pay you, you know, Mrs. Garvey."

"Yes, I know. Use it anyway."

He tapped in Info and Connection, and waited.

"Hello, uh yeah. I'm doing a school project and I wondered if you could tell me the name of the storyteller on the DV show that aired tonight?"

"Sure, but why should I, kid?"

"Are you the voice off camera he's always talking to?"

"Yeah, yeah. So what?"

"You guys are good. Funny. I mean, you make a good team."

"Yeah, yeah, ha, ha. Listen, the guy's name is J. Adam. Anything else?"

"Do you know where he lives?"

"No way, kid! Even if I did, which I don't, I'd lose my job giving that one away."

"Well, thanks."

"Yeah, yeah, but I didn't tell you nothing. Got it? Nothing, and don't go coming around here neither. I'll kick your butt if I catch you hanging around here."

Jake hung up and began to work.

Morning came, but the DV screen said:

PROGRAM DELAYED UNTIL TONIGHT

CHAPTER 4

Jake walked through the school gate on time.

"This is a first, Jake," Alvin said. "Congrats."

"Thanks," Jake said and smiled.

A couple of kids nudged each other as he walked casually into the school, but what did he care? A dark-haired girl walked up and punched him gently on the arm like she knew him.

"It's me, Jake. Mellie. How do you like it?"

She was dressed cute in a tight, red skirt, hair straightened out and cut real short, and she'd lost the earrings.

"Uh, good. Real good," he answered, tongue-tied and thinking now she was Pretty Mellie.

"Pa forked out for it. He said I wasn't never getting married-up looking the way I did. Said I could be cute. Do you think I'm cute now, Jake?"

"Yeah, sure. Cute, real cute, I guess, but I liked the old Mellie."

"Me too, but thanks anyways, Jake. My pa's gonna introduce me to some guy, to get dowry. You know," she said apologetically, smiling weakly.

"Dowry? Married? Don't do it, Mellie. You're too young. You got smarts! You gotta finish school," he said, recognizing Mrs. Garvey's message to him.

"I don't got no say, Jake. He's planned the first date for tonight."

"Date?"

"You know, a trial meeting."

"Don't go. That ain't no date. He's selling you."

"I got to, Jake," she said sadly.

"Tell him you got a date already. Come home with me. We can have some popcorn and watch DV."

"You mean that storyteller guy?"

"Yeah, you watched him too?"

"It was a good show, excepting Pa cut it off before it was over."

"It's supposed to be on again tonight. Come on, come watch with me and Evan."

"You really want me to, Jake? Won't your ma be upset, you bringing a girl home?"

"My ma ain't gonna say nothing cause she left us, and I'm sure Mrs. Garvey won't mind. Me and Evan, we're staying with her for a little, til I figure what to do."

"Oh Jake, I wanna come, but my pa'll be too mad."

"Tell him, tell him I'm a real rich Gizmo kid."

"But that's a lie."

"Sure, but how's he gonna know? It's better than letting your old man sell you so he can booze the money away. And I'll bet he never marries you off. Then he couldn't get no more money."

"It ain't his fault. It's cause Mama died. It made him so sad, but he still loves me."

"Yeah, well maybe, but what kinda love is that, Mellie? Come on, come home with me. Please, Mellie."

She finally nodded. While he was in Old Ap's class it struck him that a girl kind of liked him.

"Mr. Law-rence. Your assignment please," Mr. Ap-pel said with his hand out.

"Sure," he said. "Here."

"Thank you," Mr. Ap-pel said with a little smile.

After class, Jake stopped at Old Ap's desk a minute.

"Surprised, wasn't you, Mr. Ap-pel, that I had done it?"

"Actually, pleased is a more apt description. Now then, the interview is due in six weeks. It should be at least seven pages if computer processed or fourteen if handwritten."

"Geez, I can't think of that much to ask!"

"Well, you had better start thinking. Now hurry, or you'll be late again."

"Thanks a lot," Jake muttered as he ran down the hall to his next class.

A glimpse of Mellie in the lunch room made him smile. He saw something that made him smile more. Other guys were looking at Mellie. Too late, he hoped. His pleasure turned to nerves as Mikel Partont stopped her. Jerk! He'd never even said hi to Mellie before. What was he butting in for now?

The day finally ended. Jake felt his stomach spasm as he waited for Mellie. What did he expect? He may have talked to her some before, but he'd never given her much thought. Still, he hadn't been playing with her when he'd invited her to come home with him. He didn't want her to end up Pretty Mellie.

After a few minutes, his hopes began to sink. After a few more, he was heading for the gate when he heard her call.

"Jake, wait," she said breathlessly. "I was afraid you woulda left. I hadda leave the message for my Pa, and then Mikel kept bugging me, so Mr. Ap-pel lectured me 'bout staying away from Mikel cause he was trouble, which I already knew, and, well, I'm glad you waited!"

"Sure, me too."

She was flushed and the color on her pale cheeks looked good. They passed Alvin, who openly winked, which made him blush, the heat from it crawling up his face.

The sky suddenly let loose with a light drizzle that increased into a steady drum of rain. He hated the rain. It always came down mixed with dirt, the slushy muck sticking to everything.

"We could run," Mellie suggested.

"Naw, this stuff is too slick, sides running makes you look scared, which ain't such a good idea around here. Your neighborhood's better than this, huh?"

"Yeah, a little. We ain't got much, but let's just say I told a bigger lie than I thought when I said you were a rich Gizmo."

"Are you sorry yet?"

"Not yet," she said.

He nodded. He wasn't going to make her sorry either. His own grimy building reared up out of the jumbled architecture that twisted between the pipings. He pushed his way in and hurried up the dark stairs, hoping Mellie wasn't too freaked.

"I gotta check and see if Ma is back before we go across to Mrs. Garvey's. Wait in the hall a minute."

Course his ma wasn't there. He turned to leave, almost in relief, and Mellie was standing there inside the doorway, with her mouth open.

"This is where you live?"

He hung his head. "When Ma's around," he muttered. "Come on, it's nicer across the hall." He paused. "Are you sorry yet?"

She looked around, drew in a deep breath and said, "No, Jake. Where you live, that ain't you. Don't matter."

Mrs. Garvey gave them a big smile, a glass of milk and a bowl of berries, white with powdered sugar.

"This is nice," Mellie said. "What's a rich lady doing in this building?"

"She ain't rich no more," Jake said.

"No? Then how's she afford berries?"

He shrugged. Evan wandered in in his aimless way, groggy from a nap. "Hey, guy," Jake said, reaching out and drawing him into his lap. He popped a berry in his mouth and wiped the drip of juice off his chin.

HE SHRUGGED EVAN WANDERED IN IN HIS AIMLESS WAY GROGGY FROM A NAP "HEY GUY,"

JAKE SAID, REACHING OUT AND DRAWING HIM INTO HIS LAP. HE POPPED A BERRY
IN HIS MOUTH AND WIPED THE DRIP OF JUICE OFF HIS CHIN
"EVAN THIS IS MELLIE," HE SAID KISSING HIS BROTHER
"HI EVAN" SHE SAID
"HE'S PLAGUE DAMAGED, MELLIE, BUT SOMEDAY, I SWEAR, HE'LL TALK"
"I HOPE SO" SHE SAID SOFTLY, AS SHE WATCHED EVAN STUFF BERRIES IN HIS MOUTH UNTIL HIS CHEEKS BULGED
"WELL, AT LEAST HE KNOWS WHAT HE LIKES" JAKE SMILED, WIPING HIS FACE AGAIN
MRS. FARLEY TOOK EVAN TO THE SINK AND SAID "WOULD YOU HAVE DINNER WITH US, MELLIE"
"THANKS, I'D LIKE THAT" MELLIE ANSWERED
"JAKE" MRS. CARVEY WHISPERED "WHAT'S SHE DOING HERE"
"SHE'S HIDING FROM HER PA HE WANTS TO DO AWAY HER OF IT"

"Evan, this is Mellie," he said, kissing his brother.

"Hi, Evan," she said.

"He's Plague-damaged, Mellie, but someday, I swear, he'll talk."

"I hope so," she said softly, as she watched Evan stuff berries in his mouth until his cheeks bulged.

"Well, at least he knows what he likes," Jake smiled, wiping his face again.

Mrs. Garvey took Evan to the sink and said, "Will you have dinner with us, Mellie?"

"Thanks, I'd like that," Mellie answered.

"Why don't you go in the back room with Evan and turn on the DV," Mrs. Garvey suggested, "while Jake and I clean up."

"Sure," Mellie said.

"Jake," Mrs. Garvey whispered, "what's she doing here?"

"She's hiding from her pa. He wants to dowry her off."

"But she couldn't be more than fourteen."

"Yeah, I know and she's smart, but her pa wants her to be Pretty Mellie, not just Mellie."

"What do you mean, Jake?"

"Never mind."

"Listen honey, her father could make big, big trouble for you."

"Maybe, but what else could I do? I had to help her," he said.

"Hurry, the storyteller's coming on," Mellie called.

CHAPTER 5

Colony classes began when they were thirteen. The teachers summoned them to the observatory deck. All around them the walls were thick, clear plastic, crisscrossed by silver beams. Outside surrounding, engulfing them was the black space between worlds.

The teacher was not what they had expected. He looked like none of them. His head was leonine, his hair a purple halo around his face, his body sleek and unclothed.

"Yuck," a boy said.

"That is not an appropriate response," the teacher said.

"But you are ..."

"Yes, to you, I am."

"Why are you here?" another student asked. "You are not one of us."

"Aha," the teacher responded, his body suddenly sliding back into his true shape. "Now I am," he said. "You see, I was not what I seemed and another species might not be either. They might view us as you just viewed me. You are dismissed."

"Wait," Acob cried. "How did you do that?"

The teacher looked up. "You are determined to know, and you will, but not today. Today you will answer another question. How do you know what someone really is?"

"I know," a girl said, waving her hand. "By what they tell other people."

"Perhaps. Anyone else?"

"By what they do and how they treat others."

"Perhaps. Anyone else."

"Perhaps you never know," Acob said. "It would seem hard to tell, especially if you could change shape."

"That's an interesting idea," the teacher said, "but why would your shape matter?"

"I'm not sure," Acob said, feeling disconcerted. "But, it must."

"Oh," the teacher said again, and slid into a new form. This

time he was a squat, little man, with knobby protrusions on his back and too many fingers on his hands.

"Why do you do that?" Acob asked.

"Why do you think?"

Every class ended with another question. Every class left Acob more and more uneasy. Then one day, the teacher said, "Today you will each pretend to be someone else."

"Why?" a boy asked.

"Just try it. Your question will partly answer itself."

They all tried and nothing happened.

"We can't," they said.

"Can't what?" the teacher asked.

"Be someone else, obviously," Acob said.

"Not yet, but you will learn."

Timiial came forward. "Can I try once more?"

"Of course."

She stood, dropping her hands to her sides, stillness coming across her, her eyes closed. Acob watched, a panic seeping into him. Still, Timiial stood.

Her eyes snapped open. "I couldn't."

"Of course not," the teacher said. "You didn't know who to become."

"Aw, no," the off-camera voice broke in. "We've gone overtime! They're gonna dock my pay. Why'd I get stuck with being your tech man, old man? Why?"

"I have no idea. And I, why did I get stuck with you?"

"You crazy old nut. This is gonna be my last night assigned to you, even if I hafta quit this job."

The screen went black.

CHAPTER 6

Jake and Mellie blinked.

"Why do they end it like that?" Mellie asked.

"I'm not sure they plan it. It seems like a screw up," Jake said.

"Well, it's a shame," Mellie said. "It sorta ruins the mood."

"Yeah, but I'm kinda getting fond of the camera man."

"Without him I guess we'd probably get completely sucked outta reality. I ain't never seen a DV like this. I mean, the guy takes over my mind just by talking," Mellie said.

She was right. The old man was weaving a spell that called them back to his show eagerly each night.

"I'm glad I don't go to Acob Dam's school," Mellie said suddenly.

"It ain't a school for humans. Acob Dam and his friends wouldn't wanna come to our school neither, you know, Mellie."

"I suppose not. Listen to us! Sitting here talking like those alien kids are real people."

"Yeah, we are, ain't we? They seem real. I can almost believe they're out there somewhere," Jake admitted. "I bet the DV station didn't plan on giving us no show we actually liked. Why do we like it, Mellie?"

Mellie shook her head, palms up, palms open.

"Well, I'm gonna find out. All I gotta do is get the storyteller's address and then go get Old Ap's interview. When I do, I'm gonna find out how that old man works his voodoo on us."

"I hope it ain't a DV trick," Mellie whispered.

"Why don't you look in the phone book for this Mr. Adam's address?" Mrs. Garvey asked.

"Phone book? What's a phone book, Mrs. Garvey?"

"Here you go, Jake," she said handing him a thick paper volume. "They used to make these every year. Then too few people could afford a phone, so they only make them on disc for Gizmos now. This one is really out of date, but take a chance. Maybe the storyteller is in there. It's hard to tell his age, but he doesn't look young, so maybe he had a phone when this was made and he was listed. I'm in there."

The frail pages were lined with list after list of name after name on street after street. Streets he'd never heard of, streets with names like Jolly Way and Sycamore Stand.

"Some of those streets don't exist anymore," Mrs. Garvey said, "and some are out there with no one living on them."

"Why?" Jake asked.

Mrs. Garvey shrugged.

"Wow, how do you use it?" Mellie asked, flipping the pages.

"Well, the names are alphabetical. Let's see here," Mrs. Garvey said, running her finger down the pages. "J. Adam, J. Adam. Here you go. Well, there are six J. Adams and twelve John Adams and fifteen James Adams, one Jarrad, one Jean, and three Jacobs, eight Jeffreys, four Joshuas, nine Jeremiahs. Good grief, we can't afford to call all these people. What are we going to do?"

"First we could see which of these streets are still there," Mellie suggested. "My pa has a street map the city gave him for when he's working as a garbage collector. "

"That's a great idea, Mellie," Jake said.

"Okay, I'll ask to borrow it, but right now I gotta go home."

"Maybe you should stay here the night, Mellie. It's pretty late. It might not be safe to go," Mrs. Garvey said.

"I can't. Pa'd have a fit."

"We could call him," Mrs. Garvey said.

"He ain't got a phone. I left him a message saying I was out with a rich Gizmo kid, and a rich Gizmo'd have a car to take me home in. I gotta go home, now."

"Jake, how could you do this?" Mrs. Garvey asked. "Mellie is in a lot of trouble because of you!"

"She was already in a lot of trouble. I'll take her home. She'll be fine with me," Jake bragged, and hoped he was right.

They gathered her books and jacket and left. The lights around his building had already been turned out. It was like pitch, except the rain was slick underfoot and glistened a little.

"It's spooky," Mellie said.

"Naw, it's safe long as you're with me," Jake said.

Her fingers sought his hand. They had small, rough calluses on the tips. Even so, they were nice to hold. When they got near the school, the street lights were on. Lots of guys were hanging out around the gate, chewing gum and spitting every once in a while. Two guys they knew were actually having a spitting contest, marking the distance with phosphorescent chalk.

He pressed her fingers and pulled her along quickly. He'd walked her home once before from school, but this time the distance seemed to stretch out a long way.

"Hey," someone called and then said, "what you doing with my chick, punk?" Mikel's bulky sixteen-year-old frame straddled the walk in front of him.

"She's my friend," Jake said. "Get outta our way."

"Why'd a girl pretty as Mellie wanna hang with a scarecrow like you?" Mikel spat out.

Mellie looked frightened. Her fingernails dug into the palm of his hand.

"Leave us alone, Mikel. I don't want no trouble."

HEY," SOMEONE CALLED AND THEN SAID, "WHAT YOU DOING WITH MY CHICK, PUNK
MIKEL'S BULKY SIXTEEN YEAR OLD FRAME STRADDLED THE WALK IN FRONT OF HIM
SHE'S MY FRIEND," JAKE SAID. "GET OUTTA OUR WAY
WHAT'D A GIRL PRETTY AS MILLIE WANNA HANG WITH A SCARECROW
AKE RECOGNIZED THE SLOW ANGER HE FELT GROWING IN HIMSELF. "GET OUTTA OUR W
AKE SMILED WISTFULLY. THE OTHER KID HAD HAD A KNIFE AND A RECORD SIX MILES LONG
E CAUGHT A WHIFF OF SOMETHING THAT SMELLED OF THE SWEET SHAMPOO HIS MA HAD USED

"You're the one who's gonna be leaving me and Mellie alone, Scarecrow," Mikel snorted. "Get lost and leave the beauteous lady with me."

Jake recognized the slow anger he felt growing in himself. "Get outta our way," he said again.

"You gonna make me, Scarecrow?"

"If I have to."

"Hey," Elvis Park called out. "Mikel, leave him! He's bad news."

"Sure, and I'm scared," Mikel laughed.

"You should be," Elvis said. "He nearly killed a kid when he was nine. He fights vicious."

"Gimme a break," Mikel said, almost laughing.

Jake smiled wistfully. The other kid had had a knife and a record six miles long, so Jake had walked.

"Come here, sweet, Pretty Mellie. Come to Mikel, right over here."

The creep beckoned arrogantly with one finger, ignoring Elvis' warning.

"Forget it, Mikel," Jake said.

He caught a whiff of something that smelled of the sweet shampoo his ma had used on her silky, long hair. Suddenly he was tired of the banter.

"Outta our way, now," he demanded.

Mikel sauntered up to him and Jake lost it. He took two fingers and stabbed, fast, street hard and Mikel fell back, grabbing his eyes. Jake jerked Mellie's hand and walked cooly by without looking back.

"Did you blind him?" Mellie asked, tears in her voice.

"He asked for it, Mellie, and he got it. On the streets you get whatcha ask for. If I wanna survive, I don't think about it too much. I just react, and if I need to, I run."

"But..."

"Ain't no buts. Mikel mighta ended your pa's plans for you if I'da let him. Maybe it won't make no difference anyways. You don't think your pa protects you cause he loves you, do you? You're a commodity. Good chance inside a year you'll be a charity case in maternity, and your pa'll be a little richer if he don't drink it all up."

She pulled her hand out of his and walked silently.

"Mellie, this is my life. A ma who's gone and Evan, and it ain't likely to get no better anytime soon, anyways."

She didn't say a word more until they got to her place. Here the girders were fewer, the rain not as sticky. Their hair was plastered to their faces, their clothes soaked with grime. He turned to go.

"Jake, thank you for everything. I'll ask about the map."

He smiled. "Thanks, Mellie. We still friends?"

"Sure we are. If Pa lets me, I'll watch the storyteller in the morning. See you!"

She raced up the steps and slipped in the door.

CHAPTER 7

This time he turned on the blank screen before the show began. It came up golden, like a rising sun. A graphic followed:

TRAVELS OF A COLONY
TOLD BY
J. ADAM, STORYTELER EXTRAORDINAIRE

There was pinging music. A picture flickered on and off before it focused on the old man. The tech people for this show were truly the worst ever.

The afternoon after Timiial's attempt, a new teacher came to the star room.

"I am a master," he said. "You have moved to a second level class."

He touched a button and a wall clouded over. Worlds in a whirl of color floated across it. Songs and guttural sounds, soft squeals and peepings slid by and filled their ears.

"Why do I play these for you?" the master asked.

No one answered. The sounds and colors played again.

A boy said, "Who knows."

"That is what I asked," the master said gently. "You, Timiial, why?"

She hesitated and then said, "So we can learn who we might become?"

"Quite right. Why?"

"I don't know," she said.

"Hasn't anyone explained the purpose of 'Colony' to you?"

Everyone was quiet.

"No? Colony means that you were selected to leave home, in order to go to another world to 'colonize' it as one of their people."

"What does that mean?" Acob dared to ask.

THE AFTERNOON AFTER TIMIAL'S ATTEMPT, A NEW TEACHER CAME TO THE STAR ROOM "I AM A MASTER" HE SAID "YOU HAVE MOVED TO A SECOND LEVEL EVER CLASS" HE TOUCHED A BUTTON AND A WALL CLOUDED OVER WORLDS IN A WHIRL OF COLOR FLOATED A CROSS IT SONGS AND GUTTURAL SOUNDS, SOFT SQUEALS AND DEEP RINGS SLIDE BY AND FILLED THEIR EARS "WHY DO I PLAY THESE FOR YOU?" THE MASTER ASKED

HE COULDN'T ANSWER HE ONLY KNEW HE LONGED FOR WARM SUNLIGHT AND THE STAR "WHERE WAS YOUR HOME BEFORE COLONY TIMIAL?" IN THE NORTH WHERE WINTER NIGHTS WERE BITTER AND EXIT ALONG THE SEA "I MISS THE SUN I MISS THE YELLOW BLOG ON OUR WALLS I MISS MY TELESCOPE AND THE WOODS I LEFT BEHIND BUT YOUR ROUGH AND YOUR FUR LIE AT NIGHT I HEAR YOUR CRYING IT LIKE A PLAINTIFF WHISPER IN THE DARK"

"It means you will shift into a new identity which in most respects biologically matches the population of your new world."

"Why would the people of another world want us?" Acob asked, mystified.

The master smiled. "Myril, do you know?"

"Perhaps. Is it because they won't know we are aliens?"

"Go to your quarters now. We'll go on tomorrow," the master said without truly answering.

Acob walked over. "Timiial, do you understand?"

"No," she answered. "Well, vaguely, don't you?"

"No, and I don't want to."

"Why not, Acob?"

He couldn't answer. He only knew he longed for warm sunlight and the sea.

"Where was your home before colony, Timiial?"

"In the north where winter nights were bitter and extra long," she said.

"And would you go back, if you could?"

"No," she said flatly, "not to the darkness and the cold."

"I miss the sun. I miss the yellow bugs on our walls. I miss my telescope and the books I left behind."

"But you brought your flute. At night I hear you playing it like a plaintive whisper in the dark."

"It is not enough," he sighed.

They walked to a port together, but didn't hold hands now.

The next day the master said, "In one year we'll be near a world. You are behind in your lessons. You must work harder, be ready."

"Work at what?" Acob asked.

"Timiial knows. Ask her," the master answered.

Acob looked at her. His heart fell to his toes.

"To shift," she answered. "We must be ready to shift, like teacher."

"Not quite," the master said. "Teacher shifted only to

demonstrate. He did not remain anyone else for long. When you shift to choose a new home, it will be your last shift, not just one of many more. Now which of you will try today?"

They all did, but none could. They went to their quarters and lay in bed imagining who they might be in a year or two, or what they might choose three or four years more into space.

Acob would be seventeen in three years and he could not imagine being anyone else, then or now. "I want to go home to my parents," he said to himself. "I'll remain as I am until the ship goes home."

He closed his eyes and dreamt he was a spotted, yellow bug in a patch of sun-warmed glass.

"Timiial," he said. "I don't want to shift."

"But you will, we all will. I don't think there is a choice to remain as we are."

"I'll go home with the teachers when they return."

"No," the master told them. "We never go home. You will never go home. You were chosen for Colony. None of us, none of you can go home."

"But the masters must go home," Acob had insisted.

"No, Acob. We don't."

"Why would you leave home if you couldn't return? You had choices," Acob said.

"Why does anyone go exploring? We wanted to find new and different worlds. We wanted interesting lives. We have no regrets. You, too, will get over your longing for home, Acob," the master promised.

Never, Acob thought to himself. Never.

The screen went black. The tech man said, "Your story needs work, old man."

CHAPTER 8

Jake couldn't wait to see Mellie at lunch.

"Pa was mad," she said, holding her head sideways. "He wanted to know how dumb was I. Said he could see I hadn't been out with no rich date. My hair and clothes were covered in muck. He said no rich date woulda walked in the filthy rain."

"No map then, huh?" Jake asked.

"Here," she said thrusting a map at him. "I didn't ask him."

"You just took it, as mad as he already was?"

"Yeah, well, I was mad, too," she said as she raised her face. One side was purpled, the eye almost swollen shut.

"Geez, your pa do that?" he said, reaching out gently to touch the bruise.

"He was boozed up, that's why he did it. He said he was sorry," she said, pulling away from his fingers.

"Mellie, 'sorry' don't excuse that! Don't go back. Come stay with Evan and me."

"No, Jake. I can't. He's still my pa. Look at the map tonight and I'll put it back. He'll never know."

"Aw, Mellie, that's too dangerous. Just put it back, now. I'll find another way. It's okay."

"You keep it. Give it back when you're done. That's what I wanna do."

"Mellie, next time your pa hits you, I'll..."

"No, you won't, Jake. You won't do nothing. You can't. He's my pa. He's got rights."

That afternoon Jake pored over the map. Mrs. Garvey helped him, but lots of roads they looked for were missing on the map. They found ten, and he wrote them down next to the names from the phone book, including careful instructions about how to get to the addresses.

They folded the map up in time to turn on the DV, but the screen was blank except for a message that said:

THE STORYTELLER AND HIS TALE WILL RETURN TOMORROW

"Too bad," Mrs. Garvey said. "I was really looking forward to it. Oh dear, Evan's asleep again. You know, I'm worried about him, Jake. I think he misses your ma."

As if his ma cared about him or Evan! She'd probably be a shriveled hag before she thought of them again.

"You know, Mrs. Garvey," he said as he carried Evan to bed, tucked him in and kissed him. "I think tomorrow I'm gonna look up some of these J. Adams."

"Maybe you should call some of them first, Jake. Folks might not be very receptive to an unexpected visitor. I can't afford all the calls, but I'll treat you to five or six."

"You know, I can't pay you back, probably never?"

"Yes, so you said before, but who does an old lady like me have to call anyway?"

"Don't you got family somewhere?"

"Once I had a son. He's gone," she said sadly.

"Where'd he go?"

"I don't know. I think he's dead. He was seventeen when he vanished. The worst is not knowing what happened to him. Some mornings I actually wake up hoping that it will be the day I find out for sure that he is dead."

"Sorry," he said gently. He patted her shoulder wondering if that was how he was going to feel if his ma never came back. Maybe Mrs. Garvey stayed in this dumpy building just in case her son ever did come back. He wondered how long she'd been waiting.

She smiled and moved off to do the dishes. He went into the kitchen and said goodnight before he crawled into bed next to Evan and fell asleep. In the dead of darkness, Evan started thrashing, his body twisting, his arms swinging, fists balled up on the ends. One of them caught Jake hard, like a hammer on the eye before he got Evan's arms pinned.

"Come on Evan, easy, easy," he whispered trying to ignore the pain. "It's okay, only a nightmare."

"No," the little boy groaned in the dark.

"Evan, you talked, you talked!"

Nothing more. Not a sound. Only the buzz of empty space.

"Evan!"

Evan's eyes were open, but he didn't say anything. His lips were slack, his hands relaxed. Jake kissed him. Wishful thinking. His ma had always said, it was all wishful thinking, all of it.

Jake got up and went into the bathroom. He threw cold water on his eye and tiptoed into the kitchen. Mrs. Garvey was asleep in a chair, her long gray hair loose and tangled, patterns of white streaking its ends. He opened the refrigerator door quietly and got some ice.

"What is it, Jake?" she asked softly.

"Evan socked me one in his sleep."

"Oh my, that's going to be something by morning."

"Yeah! I was getting ice for it. Evan woulda been a helluva fighter, except for the Plague. The two of us together, we coulda whipped anyone on the streets. We coulda been some kinda dangerous!"

He rested his elbows on his knees and held the ice in place.

"Mrs. Garvey, could Mellie stay with us, permanent like?"

"What? Jake, are you and she involved?"

"Naw, course not. It's her old man. He beat her up

good. She looks worse than me. I just thought, well, that she'd be safer here."

"Jake, I learned long ago you can't change some destinies. I don't think you want her pa finding her here. I'd say you shouldn't even think about it."

"Her pa could kill her."

"Yes, he could, or you, or sell her into marriage or worse, but you can't save her, honey."

"I can try," he said.

Mrs. Garvey shook her head sadly. "Take it from an old lady, Jake, it's impossible to save anyone, even yourself. Go to bed, Jake. Get some sleep."

He left the ice in a slushy pile on the table. In the morning he had to wipe up a puddle.

CHAPTER 9

Mr. Ap-pel called them into Principal Carter's office: Mikel and Mellie and him. They looked like triplets, black-eyed triplets.

"You three have been fighting," Mr. Carter accused.

"You could hardly call it fighting," Jake said calmly.

"I told you, he just attacked me," Mikel said.

"That's a lie," Mellie said. "You threatened us."

"I never laid a hand on neither of you," Mikel denied angrily.

"Then how'd we all get the matched set of eyes?" Jake asked, quickly taking advantage of the conversation's direction to shift it all another way.

"I got no idea how you guys got them eyes," Mikel said, on the defensive.

"I don't like men who hit young ladies," Mr. Ap-pel pronounced.

"Me neither," Jake said, eyeing Mikel.

"You're all on probation. It'll be automatic suspension if there's another incident," Mr. Carter announced.

"That ain't fair," Mikel exploded. "They hit me, attacked me. I never touched them."

"Oh, give it up, Mikel," Jake said, "but I agree, it ain't fair. Mellie don't deserve probation or suspension."

"Perhaps Mellanie can be excused," Mr. Carter said. "Go on now, but you boys will talk to the state probation officer this afternoon."

"State?" Mikel asked, obviously shaken up.

Jake just shrugged. He'd been there before. Life never gave you breaks. The officer would lecture, probe, try to get into your psyche and fail because he lived on the high side of town, and it was only a charity that he came down here at all. If you were lucky, the officer would forget it, not want to be bothered, and if you weren't, he'd spend hours trying to reform you before he gave up, went home to wherever Gizmos lived, and then forgot you. Nothing to worry about.

Mellie was waiting for him. "Are you okay? I can't believe all of us had black eyes!"

He smiled. "Funny, ain't it? I'll take all bets Mikel don't bother us no more."

"Probably not, but what about you? I feel terrible. You got probation for trying to protect me."

"Not to worry. It don't mean much. I been through it before. By the way, here's your map. Did your pa miss it?"

"He ain't been home since he hit me. So no, he ain't missed it."

"You're alone? That okay with you?"

"Except when I get up for school, and it's dark, and I can hear the feet of the mice in the eaves scurrying as if there's hundreds of them."

They walked toward class.

"How'd you get your eye, anyways?" she asked.

"Oh, that! Evan accidentally hammered me in his sleep."

She smiled now. "It's a weird coincidence, ain't it?"

"Yeah, Evan socks me, your pa hits you and the school thinks we been fighting with Mikel."

"Meet me after class. I'll go to Mrs. Garvey's with you for a while, but I wanna be home so I can turn on the lights before dark," she said.

"Sure," he said, unwilling to ask what her pa might say if he came home.

Mellie was looking thin, like her baby fat was melting. It made her look older, more than cute. She had high cheekbones set in an ashen face, except for the black

bruises. She didn't wear fancy clothes or makeup, or anything, but boys were looking. He wished no one else had noticed she'd gotten pretty.

"I think everyone's staring at us, Jake," she said.

"Us?"

"Yeah, probably our matching black eyes."

"Gee, I thought it was cause you're looking so good, Mellie." He hadn't meant to say it, but there it was.

"I look good beat up?"

"Naw, that's not what I mean. You look womanly," he said, trying to explain it and fumbling it again.

"Womanly?" she said with a smile. "That's nice, Jake."

After school they walked home quietly. The blinds were drawn, casting darkness around the apartment more than usual.

"Evan, Mrs. Garvey?" Jake called, feeling panic shake him.

"In the library, Jake. At the end of the hall."

"Wow!" he said, as he and Mellie entered the room.

The walls of the library were lined in books set on shelves, stashed in boxes, heaped in piles. Soft covers and hard covers leaned into each other, sometimes held together with rubber bands, other times standing whole and intact. Embossed titles, gold lettering, bright and dark covers sandwiched precious, yellowing pages and creamy, coated papers.

"I loved books," Mrs. Garvey said. "I've been reading to Evan. He likes books too." She set the little boy down out of her lap. "When people stopped buying books you could pick them up for free, first from stores, then off the sidewalks on trash day. So I'd get up early and scour the streets, rescuing whatever I could."

"You rescued a lot," Jake said.

She nodded. "Listen Jake, I've made some calls for you, but none of the people I called were the storyteller. When school breaks Friday for early release, you should check out some more addresses. Some of the people are probably dead, others probably moved away a long time ago, but to be sure, you'll have to go to the addresses. Here's a list." She handed him a folded sheath of papers.

"Thanks a heap, Mrs. Garvey. This is a great start." He looked around again. "I didn't know nobody had real books like this in their home," he said waving his hand around the room.

"I hadn't been in here to read in a long, long time. Sitting here and reading to Evan was very comforting. Funny how a book takes you to a special place without techno-gimmicks or cyber-tricks, or anything fancy."

"Colony is like that for me, except I hear it instead of reading it, and the sounds of the story make me see the illustrations in my head," Jake said.

The room was cozy. Late afternoon light cast patches of warmth on the floors and chairs. Evan had curled up in one, his eyes moving about, watching. It was at these moments that Jake was sure he was smart.

"Let's go watch 'Travels of a Colony'. It's on in a couple of minutes," Mrs. Garvey said, pushing herself out of the chair. "Evan can stay if he wants. He likes it in here."

"Me too," Mellie said, "but I want to see the show."

"You can come back after it's over and pick out a book to read," Mrs. Garvey suggested.

"Hey, it's already begun. Those jerks, they switched the time on us," Jake shouted from the other room.

"So what's new? They do that all the time if another show is gonna make them more money," Mellie sighed.

"Shush now, just watch and listen," Mrs. Garvey said, sliding into a chair and sitting down.

And so they learned to shift, almost by accident. Timiial flowed like smooth liquid, while Mial jerked from one form to another and Wati blinked in and out. As for Acob, he didn't even try.

The first world soon hung like a sore spot in space. It was a scarlet egg with bald splotches on its tapered end.

"What kind of beings live here?" they all chorused in excitement, all gathered around the master.

"We do not know. It is possible no creatures live here at all. It is a new planet, on which no previous Colony has filed a report."

"And if there is no life?" Timiial asked.

"We will leave, but first we will send a probe to observe and see."

The probe scurried above the planet's surface. It was a palm-sized machine, mainly a camera eye and microphone, that could fly unnoticed. They were about to recall it, for no intelligent thing had become visible, when a creature darted into its line of vision. It was a slender thing adorned with four legs and one arm-like appendage. Its color matched that of the red soil with slightly darker blotches that spread across its body when it was in the shade, so that it faded into its background.

"It shifts," one of them sang out.

"Not like we do," the master said. "Only its color changes."

"Is it intelligent?" Acob asked.

"Perhaps. Let's watch a bit more."

An hour later, another of its kind came, except that it had two arms and a small set of five horns. They paced backward and of a sudden, turned and charged each other. Red dust flew up into a cloud, obscuring the creatures, and when it settled, not a living thing was visible.

"Where are they?" they asked.

The master shrugged. "Who's to know?"

The probe spent several more days searching, but found no other sign of the red creatures. It did find a glade of orange

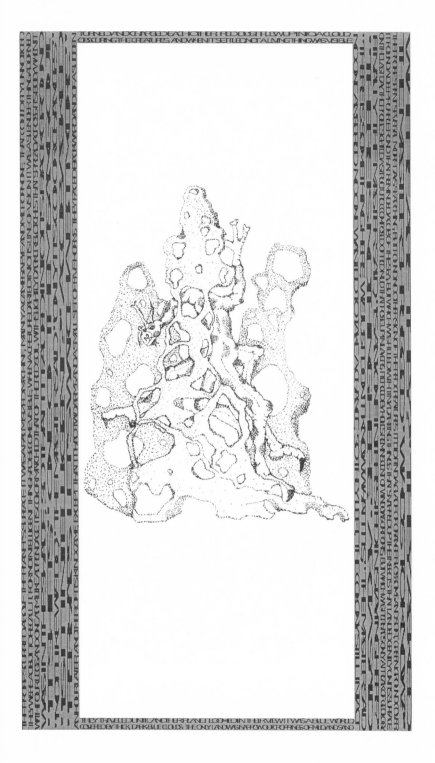

TURNED AND EXPLODED EACH OTHER. FIELD DUST FLEW UP INTO A CLOUD OBSCURING THE CREATURES, AND WHEN IT SETTLED NOT A LIVING THING WAS VISIBLE

THEY TRAVELLED UNTIL ANOTHER PLANET LOOMED IN THEIR VIEW. IT WAS A BLUE WORLD COVERED BY THICK DARK BLUE CLOUDS. THE ONLY LAND WAS NARROW QUICK-POINTING CHANNELS OF LAND AND

blossoms and soft, green ground cover. It found a deep purple pond that reminded Acob of the sea, but which was filled with tiny darting things that snapped up the insects that landed gently on its surface. On the last day, the probe sighted a structure composed of red mud that rose up in layers, pierced by holes reminiscent of windows or ports, but which was perhaps only a freak of geology.

Finally the master said, "Is anyone interested in staying here?"

"There is nothing here," Arcia said.

"There is something here, we just don't know what it is," the master said.

No one answered. No one wanted to take a chance. So they left, the Colony still intact.

They traveled until another planet loomed in their view. It was a blue world, covered by thick, dark-blue clouds. The only land was narrow outcroppings of mud and sand, haphazardly dappling the ocean surfaces. Round, portly figures sunned along the ridges, gently nuzzling each other and soaking up warmth. When a flat-bottomed boat floated near them, the rounded creatures would dive into the water, flipping over and over in a series of exotic twists, until they created waves that rolled over the boats, carrying them onto the decks. Dipping their flippers into the water, the sausage-like beings would power the boats off into the vastness of the deep, blue ocean.

"Do you think they can actually swim?" Acob asked.

"Who knows, but that looks like fun," several others said.

"What else do they do?"

"We will follow and see," the master said, sending the probe along behind a boat.

The boat floated up to platforms, built over the water, cantilevered to tremendous depth and outward from the edge of a high ridge. The platforms were piled, one over another, with spaces between, and the spaces were filled with plants and more sausage-shaped folk.

"A city," a boy remarked.

THEY TRAVELED UNTIL A OCHER RAE-IT LOOMED IN THEIR VIEW IT WAS A BLUE WORLD COVERED BY THICK DARK BLUE CLOUDS FLIPPING OVER AND OVER IN A SERIES OF EXOTIC TWISTS UNTIL THEY CREATED WAVES THAT ROLLED OVER THE BOATS CARRYING THEM ONTO THE DECKS DIPPING THEIR FLIPPERS INTO THE UNTIL A HARPOON OF A BOAT WOULD FLOAT NEAR THEM THEN THE HORNED CREATURES WOULD DIVE INTO THE THE ONLY LAND WAS NARROW VOLCANIC OUTCROPPINGS OF MUD AND SAND AND A HEAVY DRY DRIFTING THE OCEANS FLOATS ROUND FOR IDLY THE GUESS IN HEAD ALONG THE FLOES GENTLY NUZZLING

"You might be right," the master said.

"How many of these cities do you think there are?"

"Who knows, perhaps this is the only one, perhaps there are many. We will watch some more," the master said.

Two days went by during which the creatures seemed only to lounge about sunning themselves. On the third morning, a flat boat of fat, winged beings rowed up to the city. Some high pitched barks passed between them, some plants were exchanged, and an apparent celebration commenced.

"Now would be a good time for some of you to join them," the master suggested. "Who is interested?"

Most hung back, almost clinging to each other, but Myir said, "The water must be warm, the air is probably sweet. I'll go. Perhaps they have music, and if not I will teach them," she said in her song-like voice.

The next morning she was gone.

"If they can not already sing, they never will," a master said softly.

"Myir will teach them," Timiial said.

"No. Perhaps she will sing to them for a short while, but she will not be able to teach them. Soon she too will forget song. She is the one who has changed. It is she who is shifting, not them," the master said.

He left them to stand and watch through the probe's eyes, wondering which one was Myir.

"You're a downer old man. Can't you tell a happy story?" the grouchy voice grumbled.

"Next time, I promise."

CHAPTER 10

Spring weather was quixotic, sometimes hot, sometimes chilling. Friday came, as it always did, releasing Jake into an afternoon of heat. Early release, they called it, but the weather was grimy and unwelcome, and hardly offered release or relief. School might be held in an old hulk, dusky and dank, but at least an ancient air conditioner still clanged away, preventing the heat, let off when the sun hit the grime, from making the school unbearable.

Jake scurried along the walks, his eyes watchful even while his mind wandered. He had stayed up late, plotting his course for the day. The addresses were spread so far apart, he'd be lucky to get two searches done. He was taking Evan. He tried to take Evan some place on early release day. Sometimes it was too much trouble, but if he did take him, Evan liked it, Jake was sure.

He got home, trotted up the stairs and stopped. The door to Ma's apartment was agape and the rooms bare.

"Hey kid, scat," a big, brutish guy said.

"Where'd it all go?"

"Whatcha mean? That junk?"

"Yeah, that's what I mean."

"It's gone. No rent, and it's gone. Out on the street three hours ago. Probably already picked over by scavengers. Gone. Now get."

"You didn't have no right to just clean it out," Jake said, his voice wobbling at the edges of the sentence.

"Oh yeah? If it's anything to you, kid, I got law on my side. Sides, don't matter now. You see any of the junk from this rat-trap down on the street when you come up? No, cause it's gone and you're too late to get in on it!"

Gone. As gone as Ma. Wiped clean like Evan's mind. How come Evan had to be born with the Plague? Jake needed him, and who knew what Evan was thinking, where he really was, what he really wanted?

Jake took a great gasp of air and went in to get Evan ready. Maybe his ma was right all along. Maybe all his hopes for Evan only amounted to wishful thinking.

He hugged the little boy and kissed him.

"Hey, Evan, it's time to go. Ready?"

Of course, he didn't answer. Mrs. Garvey handed him Evan's hat and a bagged snack.

"Mind if I come along, Jake?" she asked.

"Naw, that'd be fine, Mrs. Garvey."

"Maybe I can help. I used to drive these streets."

"You drove?"

"Oh, yes. Long ago we all did. Now let's hurry, so we're back in time for 'Colony'."

"Yeah, let's go," he said, slamming the door behind them. Neither Mrs. Garvey nor he looked at the empty place across the hall. Evan never seemed to notice anything, but who knew, who really knew?

The Grime Effect had driven most people inside. Steam rose from the shiny gray coating, as the unwelcome and only sometimes-seen-sun struck it. Jake pulled Evan's hat down snugly on his head. With the hat on no one could see that Evan's hair, at age seven, was only thin, wiry wisps, another mark of the plague. With his hat on, people noticed Evan's big eyes and long rusty lashes. Jake was glad for the empty streets. It meant they were less likely to be hassled. He noticed how Mrs. Garvey had raised her shoulders, straightening up as if pulled by watching eyes. He peered into the windows of the towering buildings and relics, but they were empty of everything except cracked glass. He looked at Evan trotting beside him, his hand complacently clutched in Jake's.

"Well now, let me see. We're going to have to hop a public tram to St. Joseph Street," Mrs. Garvey said.

"I got no money for a tram," Jake said.

JAKE TOOK A GREAT GASP OF AIR AND WENT IN TO GET BREAKFAST. MAYBE MA WAS RIGHT.

MAYBE ALL HIS GOOD THOUGHTS ABOUT THE AIM WERE WISHFULL THINKING.

"I know, but I have a bit."

Not that the tram was much, but it was richer than he was. He wondered how much Mrs. Garvey's bit of money was? It seemed to get to be a bit more each time they needed some.

"That's real nice of you, Mrs. Garvey."

"You're the one who's doing me the good turn, Jake. It's been a long time since I had an escort to go anywhere at all."

"Yeah?" he asked.

She nodded her head.

A middle-aged gang shifted from one foot to the other, eyeing each other, muttering and grumbling every so often as they waited for the tram. Several displayed detailed tattooing, some in multi-colors, others in the standard deep blue. The Multis strutted their rank inside the gangs by the amount of detail and the number of colors they could afford. The older the gang, the more dangerous. Survival of the most brutal.

He carefully walked past them, eyes ahead, holding himself to a steady pace. Out of the corner of his eye, he noticed Mrs.Garvey following his lead. She was a pretty savvy old lady.

"We'd better try a different stop," she suggested softly.

"Too far for Evan. It's here or nowhere. Just stand quiet. If we're lucky, they won't take much note of us," he whispered back.

He picked Evan up just in case they had to take off. This bringing Mrs. Garvey along might have been a big mistake. He couldn't carry her. They settled on a low wall and waited. He'd never ridden a tram before.

"Hey, kid, lady," a gaudily tattooed bruiser said, "you waiting for the tram?"

"Yes, sir," Mrs. Garvey said.

"Where'd a kid like you get money for the tram?" he asked Jake, ignoring Mrs. Garvey now.

"My teacher gave it to me," he lied quickly, easily from practice.

"Teacher give it for the old lady and kid, too?"

"Kid rides free, and she begged hers," Jake said smoothly.

"Why's this kid ride free?" the man said, patting Evan, eyeing Jake.

"Take off his hat," Jake said, staring the man down.

The fat hand lifted the hat and dropped it. "You let me touch the Plague? You punk!" the man screamed, but backed off. "You piss-off kid." He stared at Jake, furiously shaking off his crew's hands and finally, muttering and cursing, turned away.

"What just happened?" Mrs. Garvey asked, replacing Evan's hat.

"The morons think they can get the Plague from Evan."

"They could if they haven't been vaccinated, but I'm sure they have been."

"Yeah? Well, they think no matter what, touch the Plague, it strikes you either dead or sterile, the dummies."

"At this moment, I'm glad they're afraid of Evan," Mrs. Garvey said very quietly.

The tram was crowded, mainly with Tattoos. Mrs. Garvey lifted Evan's cap and tucked it under her arm. Immediately the Tattoos around them pushed away, crowding back against others, everybody hissing, "Plague."

"You learn fast, Mrs. Garvey," Jake said with a smile.

The moisture in the air was heavy with heat by the time they got off at St. Joseph and they still had five blocks to walk to St. Simeon Street. The neighborhood was lined with row after row after row of fire-gutted, stone buildings. Scarred boards were hammered over doorways and shattered windows like dirty bandages.

"Looks like no one lives around here," Jake said nervously.

They finished the walk, but the address they sought was as empty as all the others.

"Why don't they tear these things down?" Jake asked.

"Fear, I think," Mrs. Garvey said. "This was a center of Plague, Jake."

"Really? Here? But these musta been ritzy once, being one family buildings and all, like they were."

"Years and years ago they were, but disease doesn't know who's wealthy or poor. The Gizmos set their own homes afire to sterilize them, and then moved as far from them as they could," Mrs. Garvey said, shaking her head.

"Took longer than I thought to get here," Jake noted. "We'd better head on home. Next time I go searching, I'll jump a trash truck and ride its tail. They're faster than a tram."

"Jake, that's dangerous!" Mrs. Garvey exclaimed.

"Yeah, well so's the tram."

"REALLY? HERE? BUT THESE MUST ALL BEEN RITZY ONCE, BEING ONE-FAMILY BUILDINGS AND ALL, LIKE THEY WERE."

"YEARS AND YEARS AGO THEY WERE. BUT DISEASE DOESN'T KNOW WHO'S WEALTHY OR POOR. THE GIZMOS SET THEIR OWN HOMES AFIRE TO STERILIZE THEM, AND THEN MOVED AS FAR FROM THEM AS THEY COULD," MRS. GARVEY SAID, SHAKING HER HEAD.

"TOOK LONGER THAN I THOUGHT TO GET HERE," JAKE NOTED. "WE'D BETTER HEAD ON HOME NEXT TIME I GO SEARCHING I'LL JUMP A TRASH TRUCK AND RIDE ITS TAIL. THEY'RE FASTER THAN A TRAM."

"JAKE, THAT'S DANGEROUS!" MRS. GARVEY EXCLAIMED.

"YOU LEARN FAST, MRS. GARVEY," JAKE SAID WITH A SMILE.

THE MOISTURE IN THE AIR WAS HEAVY WITH HEAT BY THE TIME THEY GOT OFF AT ST. JOSEPH AND THEY STILL HAD FIVE BLOCKS TO WALK TO ST. SIMEON STREET. THE NEIGHBORHOOD WAS LINED WITH ROW AFTER ROW OF FIRE-GUTTED STONE BUILDINGS. SCARRED BOARDS WERE NAILED ACROSS DOORWAYS AND WINDOWS LIKE DIRTY BANDAGES.

"IT LOOKS LIKE NO ONE LIVES ROUND HERE," JAKE SAID NERVOUSLY.

THEY FINISHED THE WALK, BUT THE ADDRESS THEY SOUGHT WAS AS EMPTY AS ALL THE OTHERS.

"WHY DO THEY TEAR THESE THINGS DOWN?" JAKE ASKED

CHAPTER 11

The program was on. A purple light cast lavender shadows over the old man as he began.

It took a long time to travel place to place, planet to planet, and the students began to get bored. For a while they speculated on who would leave next, or what species they would become. Lots of them shifted jokingly from one form to the next, but still Acob could not. He hung back quietly and withdrew more and more.

One day Timiial laughingly poked him and said, "Acob, you must join us. Why do you sit and mope so?"

"I can't shift."

"Of course you can. You just don't want to."

"Why can't I go home instead? Why can't we, you and I, stay ourselves? No one ever says why we can't," he insisted.

"It's too far to go home, for one thing," she answered. "You can't go back to your childhood, Acob. You are far too old."

"Go away, Timiial. You don't understand," he said.

She stroked his face briefly and shrugged, turned and left.

That afternoon the master was late. The students chattered quietly until their whisperings reached even Acob.

"Shift places with someone else," Praity said.

"No," Acob said.

"Oh come, Acob, try it. You need some fun," Miyakin said.

"No."

"Hey, nobody change into Acob," she warned, calling out softly. "He's not in on it."

Around the room there were flickerings and blinkings as the students shifted, exchanging forms with one another, giggling and smiling.

"The master approaches," someone called, his/her big teeth flashing.

"Today we will observe a new planet," the master said.

Giggle.

The master glanced around the room. "Timiial? Where is Timiial?" he asked.

No one answered. He looked about the room. No one had ever missed a lesson before.

"Is she ill?" he asked, looking again. "Where is she?"

Everyone shook their heads.

"Acob?" he said, calling on him.

Giggle. As he stood, another Acob stood.

"What is going on here?" the master asked.

"What do you mean?" the other Acob asked.

"Who are you?" the master accused.

"Acob," she/he answered.

"Ah," said the master. "This is a very old trick."

"It is?" the other Acob asked.

"Oh yes, in every set of students there is always one smart aleck who pulls this trick, but I am surprised it is you, Timiial. Please sit down."

Giggle, again.

"The joke is over," he said calmly and went on with their lesson, asking this one, that one, another one, the other Acob, questions, getting answers.

The master must have heard the giggles, but ignored them. Slowly Acob began to smile as well. The other Acob grinned back at him. They gave many odd answers that day, but the master only scratched his head. At last, without thinking, Acob shifted.

"Ah, Timiial," the master greeted Acob. "How nice to have you back," he said with a slightly triumphant note in his voice.

Acob/Timiial just smiled.

"Better," the tech man called out. "Much better. Keep it up and they might let you stay on."

"I'll try."

When did a tech man get to be a comic, Jake wondered to himself.

CHAPTER 12

Jake wished he could shape shift. He'd change into some rich dude with loads of gizmos, then just keep shifting in and out of that life, back and forth, into and out of the lives of other rich Gizmos, confusing everyone. What a fantastic joke it would be, and all the while he'd be getting really, filthy wealthy.

"And what would you do with all that money?" Mrs. Garvey asked when he mentioned it to her.

"Buy more gizmos and make more money."

"Oh, I see," she answered.

Jake thought it wasn't a very enthusiastic reply. He put Evan to bed, stroking his head, wondering how anyone could be afraid of the little boy.

"Mrs. Garvey, what would you do if you were rich?" he asked returning to the kitchen.

"Me?"

"Yeah, if you were really, really rich?"

"Well, I wouldn't buy gizmos."

"No?"

She shook her head.

"Then what would you do?"

"I don't know. So much that I might have wanted is lost forever." She sighed loudly before saying, "Why don't you choose some addresses to look for tomorrow?"

He examined the list and finally figured out what he was going to do, but kept it to himself. He slept until midnight, dressed and slipped out of the apartment quietly. He'd be back in time to give Evan breakfast. This time he'd just see which houses still stood, and if they were inhabited, before he actually tried knocking on doors.

At this hour, the streets were littered with castoffs, people even poorer than Jake. They were taking advantage of the momentary coolness of the hour in a flurry of both searching through the garbage and of trading scavenged treasures before the trash trucks came.

Jake ignored them and poised himself on a corner, waiting for a truck. He heard it before he saw it. He felt it before it came into view. It rumbled around the corner. He waited. Long, rusted, mechanical arms reached out from the back of the truck, scooping up cans and scattered junk. Rumor had it that the arms would scoop up a person as easily as a can. Rumor furthered the idea that Gizmo people never got scooped up and dumped like everyday garbage.

Jake waited. He jumped, grabbing the tail extensions, squeezing between the open compressor and an arm as it reached and pulled and dumped trash.

He knew he had to ride fifteen blocks and began counting. When he got to number fifteen, he waited, holding his breath, timing his jump, landing cat-like on the balls of his feet and rolling away. He felt the breath of an arm as it passed all too close to him. Rolling a little further, just to be sure, he finally rose to his feet.

Hardly anyone lived here and absolutely no one loitered about. It was at the border of two city sections. He walked another block and waited. This time the truck was slower and he made the jump more easily. All Streeties could move through the city on the trucks. The truck rumbled along, sweeping the streets, pulling up a bit here, a bit there, nothing huge. At block sixty-five, he jumped again.

He rolled quickly, more deftly, and waited until the truck vanished around the corner. It would return in two hours. He would have to be back here to catch it or be stranded. He looked around, got his bearings and began to walk. The streets were dark. He looked up and could see full, black sky, clear of any pipes or walls or windows. As Jake watched, night-darkened clouds glided swiftly across the round moon, and for a rare moment the edges of the clouds were outlined in golden light. He craned his neck as he walked, admiring the sky and the breeze, enjoying the safety of a deserted area until he tripped off the sidewalk, and slid out of control down a dew-wet hill.

He grappled about in the dark. He had never been anywhere without walks. A field was dimly moon-lit in front of him, bushes and grasses illuminated in shades of blackened green, hills humped and dark like the heads of sleeping monsters. He had fallen into the Dead Zone!

If the house he sought was in here, no one was living in it. Only the dead walked here, only ghosts waiting to swallow the souls of all trespassers who ventured onto their land. He was marked for death. Something dark and quick brushed softly against his legs and he screamed.

Desperately, he stumbled backwards, crouching down, searching with his hands, scrabbling around in cool blades of grass and patches of something velvety. Why could he see the stars so clearly while the walk remained invisible? The blades of grass grew sharp, scraping his fingers and palms. His heart beat staccato, drumming in his head. Perhaps he was already dead. What would become of Evan, of Mrs. Garvey?

Calm down, slow down, think! Search, he told himself, side-to-side in a pattern. Move this way, now that, now another. Don't stop, don't stop.

Time ticked away, replacing the rhythm of his heart. Minutes stretched out, pulling from him all hope of catching a truck back. His fingers were raw, and both fear and the chill were numbing him, when he stumped his toes on the walk!

He crawled onto it, heaving in gasps of living air, and forced himself up. His Streetie sense of direction carried him back towards the truck route.

CHAPTER 13

He was sure the last truck had come and gone. He huddled on the walk, wondering what to do next when he heard a rumble. He took a breath, readied himself and jumped. Chilled to the bone by ghosts, he clung and jumped, jumped again, and rode home. School was only a few hours away.

The apartment was silent when he climbed the stairs. He went into the bathroom and peered at himself in the mirror. His hair was wet with dew, his clothes flecked by tiny pieces of grass he had torn apart in his desperation. He stripped, splashed water on his face, ran its coolness over his sore fingers, and changed into clean clothes.

Ghosts had touched his clothes. He stuffed them as far under his bed as he could. He would never wear them again. He crawled into bed.

Visions of dark, shadowy things calling for him through the streets stepped out behind his eyelids every time he fell asleep. People he knew shifted into skeletons and fell apart into dust. He just called and called, "Come back, come back, don't leave me here!"

He awoke with a start. Leave him where? Groggily he wandered into the kitchen. Mrs. Garvey was humming as she made breakfast.

"We'll eat in front of the DV. Hurry now. Evan's already there."

Even though they were sitting side-by-side as they watched the show, Mrs. Garvey didn't seem to notice anything different about him.

"You ought to call this dumb show 'Shifting' or some such," the tech man grumbled into the microphone.

The storyteller just smiled.

That tech man and Jake had something in common. Mr. J. Adam was causing them both a heap of trouble.

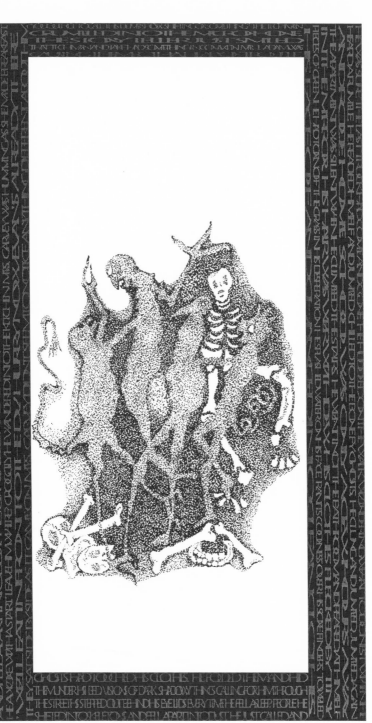

Acob had discovered he could shift, but unlike everyone else, he could only duplicate someone who already existed. He could not shift into a new biological entity as his classmates could. The master said it was an uncommon birth defect, and he might not be able to colonize anywhere.

"Why do our people become Colonies?" Acob asked, frightened of the answer.

"Someday soon, I promise to tell you, Acob. It's complicated, and today we approach another world," the master said.

This world had thinking beings, beautiful, long-haired, gazelle-like creatures, with hands for tool making. They spent their lives eagerly creating carvings and tending their young. They used the carvings for trade with other groups, embedding them into the structures they built. Ranking in the society seemed to be determined by the number of carvings a creature could trade with other groups, and then arrange into the structure of its home. Rank gave the privilege of creating more children and having first choice among mates. No one pledged to anyone else permanently, but everyone seemed to have at least two children. It was unclear who was male or female. One painting adorning a wall showed a battle, but the probe found no other signs of violence or ill health. Many students were considering this world.

While Colony observed the world, a master called Acob into his study.

"Acob, we have discussed your case. There are fewer and fewer students. Several will leave for this world we are at now. When the ship is empty, we teachers and masters will choose a place to leave you."

"But, I want to go home."

"Yes, we know, but you cannot, nor can we leave you on just any world, for you will need special circumstances in order to blend into your new home."

"This isn't fair! I should never have been chosen for Colony."

"No, but you were, and it is far too late to change that."

"At least tell me why our people go off to Colonies."

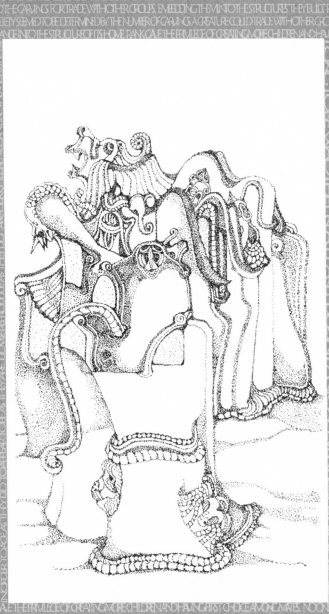

"Leaving home is a privilege, an honor, a chance to assure the survival of our race. Our world long ago exceeded its food resources as we overpopulated it. It is an old story. Wastes increased, birth defects were rampant. Strict laws were enforced. Voluntary colonization was implemented. This was long ago and it worked for a while. Things improved. Then people forgot. Birth defects increased again and colonization became mandatory. Colony evolved, became a part of our lives, assured us of survival."

"How can you claim that we of Colony survive when we do not even retain memories of ourselves? Doesn't anyone ever long to be who they really are? Doesn't anyone ever regret shifting."

"Ah, Acob, those are easy questions to answer. We are who we believe we are. When we forget who we were, we live our lives growing and aging like those around us. We believe we are whoever we shifted into, so what is there to regret?"

"But, we are not the same as they are," Acob said.

"No, but we are natural mimics. Our organs adapt, mimic theirs. We make constant, tiny shifts we don't notice ourselves in order to age as they do, to appear to be as they are."

"Do we reproduce as they do? Are our children born like them or like us? Able or unable to shift?"

"We do not know. It seems to vary from case to case, but in those cases where children are born into our true juvenile forms, they are viewed by all their parents as defective."

"What becomes of them, of those children?"

"Sometimes they survive until shift time. Sometimes they are neglected, or persecuted, or do not survive the local diseases. But many are born in the shape of their new world, as if the genes of our people are either dominated or have changed."

"I don't understand how you can call that survival," Acob still insisted.

"Acob, is it not better to shift than to die or be forever alone? Can you not take comfort in the honor of Colony?"

The honor was not a comfort. Acob went back to the students. Timiial was waiting for him.

"Five of us have chosen this world," she said. "Come, be the sixth. Be with me as you promised. I do not want to go without you. We have been friends for such a long time. Please come."

"I can't," he said sadly. "I can't, but I will remember you always."

"And I you," she said, making another promise that would be broken.

"Yeesh, can't the guy even get the girl in this stupid story?" the tech man complained.

"I cannot change the story," J. Adam, the storyteller said.

"Why not? It's just a story."

"I cannot is all. It is set."

"Well unset it. This shifting junk is way too creepy. Who'd wanna shift? Take my advice and think up a different plot, old man."

CHAPTER 14

All the kids at school were talking about *Colony.* The show was a hit, too good to be true for 2DV, weird but appealing, sad but interesting.

"Ever notice there ain't no gimmicks on 'Colony'?" Jake asked Arty.

"Gimmicks?"

"Yeah, no hi-tech, just the words and the story," Jake said.

Arty scratched his head.

"It's kinda like reading, don't you think?" Jake ventured.

"Reading?" Arty paused for half a second. "Naw, you're all wet. It's DV, Jake."

Mellie came up and said, "Jake's right, Arty. It's more like reading than DV."

"You two been hanging out together too much," Arty said.

Even Mr. Ap-pel brought *Colony* up. "I wonder what you think of the phenomenon of the storyteller on 2DV?" he asked.

Jake could hardly believe Mr. Ap-pel watched 2DV.

"Hey, Mr. Ap-pel, why you watching our 2DV shows? You must gotta have 3DV," Malcolm Barns yelled out loudly.

"Actually, I do not. I am, as you so frequently remind me, too 20th for 3DV. The fact is, I rarely watch any DV," he added.

"But you watch 'Travels of a Colony'?" Jake muttered to himself quizzically.

"Now then, let's try to evaluate this program," Mr. Ap-pel continued.

"E-val-u-ate," Malcolm repeated.

"Yes, Mr. Barns. Do you like 'Colony'?"

"I sure do. So do my little sisters, and my brothers, and my out-of-work pa. We all watches it."

"Why?"

"Cause we likes it."

"Yes, but why do you like it?"

"I don't got the vaguest." Some kids laughed.

"Mr. Law-rence, do you like it?"

The old coot already knew the answer, so Jake just nodded.

"Why, Mr. Law-rence, do you like it?"

"Cause it ain't hi-tech, I guess. When you gotta think something, it don't seem like a trick the way 3DV is. Funny, but thinking it makes it real."

"Good! Anything else? What about theme or story plot?"

"Oh, sure. The story's good. Bizarre but good. Makes a person wanna know what happens to the kids. Makes you wanna find out the ending."

"Good, good. The story is strangely compelling. We like Acob Dam and that makes us want him to win, to get to go home. The question is, will he? And, if you think about it, because the story is never finished, the show keeps us coming back and back, for more and more."

"That's cause the DV people is cheap, Mr. Ap-pel. They never lets the old man finish," Malcolm said. "They don't care if we watches or not."

"Perhaps you are right, but in that case they have accidentally created appeal. Now then, what do you think will happen if they realize we genuinely like the show?"

"Bump it upstairs to 3DV."

"Make it even shorter."

"Fire the guy?"

The answers flew about.

"Anyways it goes, they sure ain't gonna let us keep

nothing good for long," Jake murmured. He had to find the storyteller and soon, or the trail would be dead cold.

"One more thing, for tomorrow," Mr. Ap-pel added. "Your homework is to decide which of the characters in 'Colony' is right, the masters who seek a new kind of survival or Acob Dam who wants to retain his identity at all costs? And, even if Acob is right, does he know who he is any more after all the time he's spent in space and all the things he's seen? A three paragraph assignment, please."

The bell buzzed and lunch came. Mellie sat beside him sipping a drink through a newly bruised lip.

"Jake, your offer to live with you guys, it still good?" she asked.

"Course it is, but you know, my neck of the woods is real rough."

"So is mine. My pa keeps sending me out on these awful dates. There was a young guy with pitted skin and greasy fingers, and a wrinkled-up, old man who had such sour breath I gagged when he tried to kiss me. I won't kiss them, so either they hit me or Pa does later. I hate Pa. I hate them all!" She clenched her fist into a ball.

He lifted her chin to look at her lip.

"Think it'll scar?" she asked.

"Don't know. When you wanna get your stuff?"

"Today. My pa should be gone after school."

"You gonna tell him where you're going?"

"No way! I'm just gone. I never, ever wanna see him again, not ever!"

He met her after school. She took his hand. He knew she was scared. What did it mean to have a girl move into his house?

"Mellie, do you think I'm okay looking?"

She laughed. "You're beautiful, Jake, especially when you smile."

He smiled. "Then you do like me?"

"Of course."

"As a friend, or ...?"

"Oh, Jake," she said with a catch in her voice. "I can't lie to you. I don't know. I'm so confused. After all those men my pa hooked me up with, I don't want nobody to touch me."

"Okay, that's okay."

"Right now, you're the nicest person I know, Jake, and the only one I trust, but I don't know what I feel past that."

"Yeah, I guess I'm confused too. I like you, but gee, I don't got any idea what I'm supposed to think about a girl. I mean, is the liking what brings the love, or is it the sexy stuff, or what?"

She shrugged. "You're asking the wrong person. All I know is that I ain't gonna be sold to nobody, never," she stated grimly. "It's my life, not my pa's."

"I bet that's how Acob feels, too," Jake said. "He must wanna control his own life."

"Think he'll get to? Think I will?" Mellie asked.

They reached her place and climbed the stairs. She stuffed all her clothes into a long-handled bag, snatching up girl underwear, slippers, books, a little wooden box.

"That's it. Let's get outta here," she said.

"Where you going, Mellie?" her father snarled, unexpectedly standing in the door frame. "And who's this piece of trash you got with you?"

She froze and made a startled, strangled noise.

"I'm her man," Jake answered.

"Man? Man?" her father howled in laughter. "Well, Mellie's man, whatcha you gonna do now that I'm here, you street punk? You sure ain't taking her nowhere with me here."

Jake felt his ire rise. The man before him reeked of sweat and booze. Blood-shot veins marbled his swollen eyes. When he clenched his fists, his knuckles became humps of protruding bone. Blue tattoos, highlighted by scarlet dots lined his neck. He was a fearsome beast, but all Jake felt was a cold, growing fury.

"Walk out, right past you," he answered very, very calmly, too calmly, pushing Mellie, her bag slung over her shoulder, towards the door.

Her father let her pass.

"Don't need to stop her, just you," he said.

He backhanded Jake fast, very fast and sent him flying against a wall. A gasping moment of pain and Jake rebounded, rolling to his feet. His hand went to his knee and he jerked out his blade.

"Try it again and I'll puncture you," Jake hissed.

"The little man has a knife. Come on boy, try it."

Jake stood, his calm anger unbroken. The man charged and Jake slashed, drawing a trickle of deliberate blood down the man's cheek that fell onto his shirt to match the red dots on his neck. The man's arms raised up in reflex and Jake ducked and rolled, landing beyond the door, but not quite counting on the stairs. He stumbled, tried to recover and tumbled down the steps, a tangle of arms and legs.

He heard the man, half stamping, half stumbling down the stairs, and felt Mellie pulling at his arm. His knife was stuck firmly into his own foot where it had landed, pinning him. He pulled it and screamed, forced himself up, barely getting outside before her father. A street cleaner rounded the corner.

"Listen to me, Mellie, we gotta jump it," he gasped as he yanked her into a leap behind him, dragging her up as her father jerked to a halt under a spray of chemicals. They were safe.

"Jake," she whispered, "he almost killed you."

"But he didn't, now did he? Let's get offa this thing next turn when it slows." The smell of chemicals was burning his lungs and making him gag.

They jumped not far from home, which was good because his foot was leaking, his vision blurring, and he was not likely to walk very far.

"Do you think he'll find us?" Mellie asked.

"Maybe. Why didn't you tell me he was a Tattoo, Mellie?" he said, slurring his words. Something sticky dripped into his mouth.

"I was too embarrassed," she whispered.

"You should have told me," he said, his tongue feeling heavy.

"I'm sorry, so sorry! I thought if you knew, you wouldn't of helped me, and I didn't have nobody else but you, and I know everybody's afraid of Tattoos. When Pa was at the school, he always covered the marks and he never let it in the house, til now." It was a downpour of anguish, punctuated by her ceasing to move.

"Mellie, gotta keep moving right now," he said, weakly pulling her along by the hand. "Can't stop out here, no matter how much I wanna."

At last he found an old Streetie hiding place where he felt safe, and they squeezed in to catch their breath.

"Mellie," he said to the sobbing girl, concentrating to form the words. "It don't really matter, excepting Tattoos are terrified of the Plague, and now that I know your Pa's a Tattoo, we don't got no worries cause of Evan. If he does find us, all you gotta do is be holding Evan, and he won't want you no more. You'll be damaged goods, beyond redemption."

She looked up at him, her eyes still watery, but her sobbing was slowing. "That's okay by me," she said. "Fact is, that's just perfect by me."

CHAPTER 15

By the time they wended their way home, his knife at the ready, her bag dragging, bump-a-thump, they were exhausted and both his face and foot were swollen.

"Jake!" Mrs. Garvey cried. "Sweetie, what happened? Come in, come in. You too, Mellie. In, now!"

Jake fell into a chair and watched blood drop, plop by plop, on the upholstery. Mrs. Garvey ran about looking for stuff.

"She calls you 'sweetie'," Mellie said half wistfully, half in clear disbelief. "Nobody never called me that!"

Evan came crawling into his lap.

"Hey, Mrs. Garvey," Jake called hoarsely. "You better bring needle and thread. This foot needs ..."

"Stitches," she finished. She had a soft, worn, black bag in her hand which she opened with a snap. She pulled out all kinds of supplies.

"I wish I still had an antibiotic, but I don't anymore. This may hurt," she said, pouring something over his foot. She sewed him up neatly with tiny stitches and clipped it tight. She moved to his face.

"A few here, too," she announced.

Mellie took Evan in the other room and turned on the DV. Jake could hear the storyteller.

Timiial left, but Acob was not sad. She had been lost to him already, even before the masters had realized he was imperfect. She wanted the change. He could not, did not want it. The masters began guiding the ship in a new direction. More and more students chose to colonize worlds.

One day the masters were in a dither. "How could this have happened?"

"We weren't paying attention. We just were not alert."

"What?" Acob asked.

"What, what?" each student added, until they were all gathered and the masters finally, painfully explained.

"You will no longer be allowed to cross-sexually associate. We have been too slow to colonize you and this has happened!"

"Why not? Why? What? What has happened?"

Under a wall of protest, a master explained. "Two of you have produced a child."

"How? How?"

"Aria and Akel have had the nodes you carry on your sides break off and join. When the nodes join a child is formed. It takes only a few moments."

"Why is that so terrible?" Acob asked.

"The breaking of nodes prevents shifting to a final form. When we reach a certain age, we can choose our final, adult form. Naturally, at home, we choose to shift into the adults of our own species. The adult stage of our lives is the only time we can safely have children. On Colony you choose an alien life form as your adult form, but, no matter what life form you choose, children must be made after that last shift or the consequences are terrible."

"What will happen to Aria and Akel since they had not made this last shift?"

"They will perish. If the nodes are broken before we are in our last stage, we die."

"You should have taught us," one of the students accused. "Then this wouldn't have happened."

"We were remiss," the masters moaned. "We deliberately delay making our last shift until all of our students are placed, and the ship is dying, so even though we are older than you, and in many ways wiser, sex has not been a part of our lives. We simply did not know how to explain it to you."

At first Acob wondered what would become of Aria's and Akel's child. While everyone else planned their futures, he found himself drawn to the baby. He felt some of the innocence he longed for when he played with her. More and more he became her caretaker. Her parents wandered about in a daze, ignoring the child until one day they were found clutching each other, dead, their forms agonizingly caught by death in the middle of an attempt to shift.

"Tragedy, oh tragedy," the masters moaned. "What else can befall us?"

Acob loved the child, and the masters were content to let him care for her. She was sweet and alert. She played on his old flute with a brilliance he had never had and made even the masters calm. When he bathed her, she splashed him and made bubbles in the water. He felt love for her as a brother to a little sister.

"Why can't I take her with me when you leave me on my new world?" he questioned the masters.

"She would not survive, but she would be noticed."

"Then take us home," he tried once more.

"We cannot. It is too late," a master said softly. "Do not love her too much, Acob, for you will have to leave her behind."

"She could come with me. I could hide her."

"She would die of disease. She will be too young for her body to protect her," the masters repeated.

"Please," he begged.

Their shaking heads haunted his sleep side-by-side with her smiles and bubbles.

"Yea gawds, now you're making me cry. Just let the kid live," the tech man complained.

"I cannot just let her live," the storyteller said.

"You're the one making it up, old man. Let the kid live."

"I am making nothing up. The story is simply being told as it happens."

"So, the kid dies?"

"I have not gotten to that part."

"So, maybe she lives?" the tech man persisted.

There was no answer, but Mrs. Garvey had finished

the stitches and dressings, and Jake felt too groggy to even hobble in and join Evan for bed. At 5:45, Mrs. Garvey shook him in the chair where he had slept.

"Jake, school day."

He had to go. If he got locked out, it was the end of school for him. They wouldn't let him back in. It was the law. It was the one, unbreakable rule. Mellie helped him dress and he noticed he wasn't quite as bony as when he had moved in with Mrs. Garvey, who today gave him juice and tea and a soft egg for breakfast because he could barely chew.

"Now listen, you two, if you have any problems, you give the school my number. I'll come take care of it," she said, giving Jake a slip of paper.

"What about 'Colony'?" Jake mumbled numbly, his face swollen and awkward.

"It's not on this morning. The announcement said the storyteller didn't show up."

"Probably the tech man didn't," Mellie said. "He's a grump."

"He surely is. Too bad about that child, though," Mrs. Garvey said.

Jake thought of Evan. Too bad about Evan, too.

CHAPTER 16

Alvin had his finger on the button when he saw them. He waited to close the gate.

"Good golly, what happened to you?" he asked. "I really thought you'd missed the lock-in this time."

Jake managed a lopsided smile and a thank you as Alvin punched the buttons and the gates banged shut behind them.

Mr. Ap-pel was already lecturing when Jake hobbled into his class and slid into a chair at the back.

"Mr. Law-rence, after class, please. Now then, did anyone notice, 'Colony' was canceled this morning?" he continued.

"It'll be back," Malcolm pronounced.

"Perhaps, but can anyone think of a way to make sure of that?" He paused and waited. "No? Well, today's assignment is to write a persuasive letter to the DV station. What does 'persuasive' mean, Mr. Martin?"

"We tells them they better put it on or else!"

"No, that is threatening."

"Can't that be persuasive?" Allen giggled.

"Sometimes, but probably not in this case. We have few consequences with which to threaten them. How about you, Mr. Law-rence, any suggestions?"

He could barely keep his head up, his jaw ached, his face was swollen and Mr. Ap-pel wanted not an answer, but a ..., "Reason," he accidentally blurted in frustration.

"Good, very concise. We use reason," Mr. Ap-pel commended him.

If he could have, Jake would have laughed and hard. Instead he felt dizzy for the rest of class. He scribbled a rotten and probably unpersuasive letter, and dumped it on the pile when the buzzer for the next class beeped.

"Mr. Law-rence, have you been fighting again?"

Jake sank into a chair. His words were mushed, but he managed, "No, surviving. You ever need to survive, Mr. Ap-pel?"

The teacher stared a moment and said, "You're excused to the nurse."

The nurse let him lie down.

"Whoever stitched you up is a good doc. You can stay here as long as you want. I'll give you some antibiotic and aspirin."

He closed his eyes. His mind wandered to his search. Where would someone in hiding live? Jake didn't know why, but he was sure the man they called the storyteller didn't want to be found. It was disconcerting how the old man told the story as if the events were set, even though he was obviously making it up. That was part of the hook, the gimmick. When the storyteller acted like he believed his own tale, his listeners believed too. The old man was smart and his style took imagination. Street yarn-spinners were never that clever. They were just re-tellers, repeating and retelling and retelling. J. Adam, Storyteller Extraordinaire, had to have time to dream, to plot and plan, and dream again. That was a luxury, and luxury meant safety. Gizmos were safe, but J. Adam was no Gizmo. A Gizmo would never just tell a story without using techno-gimics. They'd use special effects and cyber stuff and VR. No, J. Adam was someone who had found a safe hiding spot. But, if he had such a place, why had he exposed himself on the DV? If Jake ever found a safe hiding spot himself, he'd never come out.

His mind was spinning wildly now. He whirled away into sleep and came out of it in a dizzying tumble of thought. The nurse was shaking him.

"We notified the lady at the number on this paper from your pocket. You're going to hospital for a few days, but not to worry, you can come back to school."

"Can't go," he mumbled numbly.

"Why not?"

"Not going. Got to take care of Evan and Mellie."

The nurse was shaking her head when Mr. Ap-pel arrived. They whispered a moment.

"Mr. Law-rence, I promise to see that Melanie gets home to her father every afternoon."

"No," he groaned. "Not there. Home to Mrs. Eloise Garvey."

"Mrs. Garvey?"

"We live at her place now, Mellie and me. She's my neighbor."

"Just a moment here, Mr. Law-rence. Your place? Mellie is living at your place?"

"Please," he begged. "Please."

"Who is Mrs. Garvey, Mr. Law-rence?"

Now the nurse broke in. "Dr. Eloise Garvey? Is that who stitched you up so neat, Jake? Are you talking about Dr. Eloise Garvey?" She was very excited.

"Dr. Garvey?" Mr. Ap-pel asked. "The same Dr. Garvey who discovered the cause of the plague that led to the vaccine?"

"It has to be," the nurse exclaimed. "Is it, Jake?"

He shrugged. "Just Mrs. Garvey's all I know. She's taking care of me and Evan and Mellie, that's all."

"But, Mellie has a father and you have a mother," Mr. Ap-pel pointed out.

He'd punched a hole in a can of worms and they were all squirming out.

"To Mrs. Garvey," he insisted painfully.

CHAPTER 17

Mrs. Garvey came. "Yes, I am now responsible for both Jake and Mellie."

She looked different. Dressed in a tailored suit, her hair pulled back into a tight knot, she seemed focused and sharp, as she kept a gentle grip on Evan's hand.

"But, Dr. Garvey, you have no legal claim," Mr. Carter, the Principal, was saying.

"No, but I have favors owed me and I will use them, I promise you. One way or another, Jake is to the Hospital and Mellie comes home to me each day."

"Dr. Garvey, I ..."

"Listen, Mr. Carter, I understand your predicament, but rules are not always just. These children are in need. Evan is very frail, Jake is all alone, and Mellie's father beats her and very nearly killed Jake. I have been a recluse in hiding for years. I simply want to be left alone. Aside from the favors I can call in, if you send Mellie back or tell her father where she is, in all likelihood we will become statistics on your conscience. Now then, tell me, it is decided, isn't it?"

"Lordy," Mr. Carter breathed, "you certainly deserve your reputation."

Something was wrong. Mrs. Garvey was so tough. Days later, as his head cleared, he was sure he had hallucinated it. Wishful thinking.

Not too many Streeties survived to a hospital and Jake was sure no Gizmos came to this one. It was sparsely furnished and sparsely staffed by a curved and shrunken man, who pushed a broom around and washed soot stained windows with vinegar and crumpled newspapers. Newspapers were expensive, out of Jake's purchase grasp, but here the most recent editions were carelessly wadded and tossed into soggy heaps.

Nobody visited him and he worried over Evan and

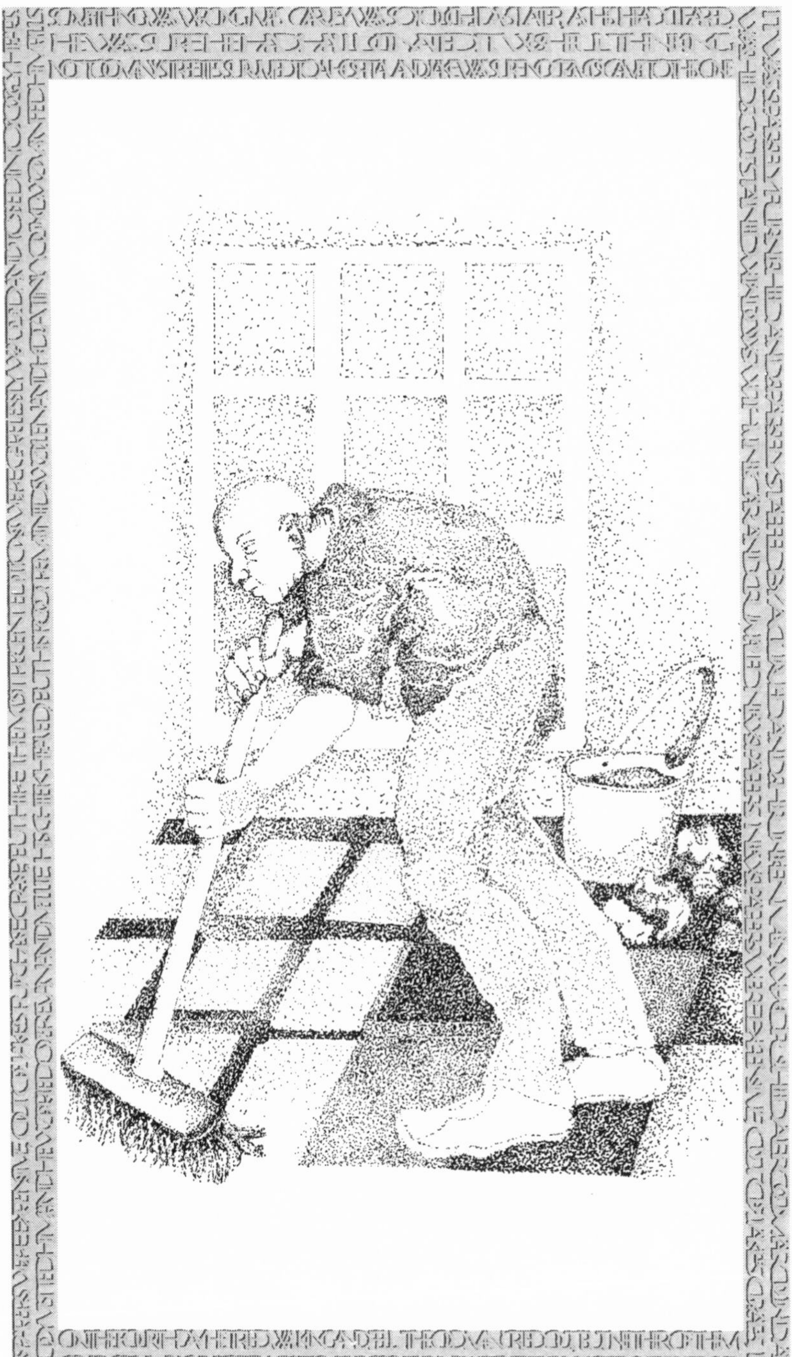

Mellie. His cheek healed, but his foot remained swollen and hot. A tiny, young woman fed him pills and juice, but he never saw a doctor, neither human nor automated.

On the fourth day he tried walking and fell. The old man cried out, but neither of them could get him back into bed. He sat on the cool tile and watched the sun creep over the floor in spots like little yellow bugs. It reminded him of *Colony*. He wanted to go home. Mrs. Garvey finally came.

"How are you?" she asked in her frumpled, familiar way.

"Not so good. Let me come home."

"In a day or so. The DV hasn't put 'Colony' back on. Mr. Ap-pel's class is petitioning. Mellie misses you," she said, ignoring his plea as she gave him all the news.

"What about Evan?"

She sighed. "The same, sweet thing that he is."

"Mrs. Garvey, you ain't no doctor, are you?"

"Do I look like a doctor? Good lord, Jake, you know me," she said, pointing an old finger at herself like a tangible question mark.

"Is Mellie still living with you?"

"Of course, for as long as she wants. Don't you know? Stray children have become my game," she smiled.

He dozed off thinking of her old-lady smile compared to his confused recollections of her in Principal Carter's office.

Eight days later he went home. His foot was tender, his face still black and blue, actually turning green now. Evan was still Evan. Jake hugged him and he hoped the boy was hugging back. Mellie came home and really hugged him. He hobbled on crutches and knew the next day he'd have to go to school. As he went to bed, he slipped a knife band onto his good leg, just in case.

CHAPTER 18

"School morning, Jake," Mrs. Garvey said gently.

He opened his eyes to the early morning darkness. Mrs. Garvey handed him his crutches and guided him to the shower. The water careened off his body in gentle spits and splotches, soothing his stiff muscles. He dried off enough to slip into his clothes and hobbled out to breakfast. Oatmeal with raisins and brown sugar was at his place. Mellie was spooning some into Evan's mouth. His little eyes seemed slacker and he drooled oatmeal back over his lip without expression. Mellie wiped his chin.

"Our petition was mailed yesterday," she said. "You think it'll work, Jake?"

"Maybe. Hope so," he said, watching Evan.

"Mr. Ap-pel gave you an extension on your interview cause of being sick and all," she told him, wiping Evan's chin again.

"Nice of him. How's Alvin?"

"Same. Said to say 'hi ya' to you," she said.

"Yeah? You almost ready to go, Mellie?"

He slid into his jacket, wishing he didn't have to go back today. The gray was just evaporating into morning as they left.

"Jake, they gotta put 'Colony' back on DV. I wanna know what happens so badly it makes me ache," she said. "If the petition don't work, then you and me gotta find Mr. Adam!"

"Aw, Mellie, don't count on nothing. The class's got a better shot at getting the show back than I got to find him with this leg and all. I ain't in any condition to go on a search."

"Don't say that, Jake. I didn't wanna tell you yet, but things took a turn at school while you been gone."

"A turn? Whatcha mean?"

"Mr. Carter got moved to another school, and this real grinder took his place. He swears he's gonna whip the school into shape or wipe us off the map. He made all the teachers report the assignments they'd given out, and any kid who don't turn them in on time is outta school. He says the government is sick and tired of carrying people along who don't come to nothing. Mr. Appel faked your due date, but you still gotta find the storyteller real soon!"

"I owe Old Ap one. You know, Mellie, I never thought about it much, but I must wanna go to school."

"There ain't nothing else," she agreed.

"Yeah, except the street. How come these Gizmos think they got the right to take school away from us? Maybe they want us to kill each other off out here."

They were on the street now. It was chilly in the shadows of the buildings. He thought of sun-yellow bugs on warm, glass window panes.

"Hospital gets more sun than the streets. Guess they want you to die in a nice place," he said.

"I'd rather live in a nice place," Mellie said.

"Mrs. Garvey's place is pretty nice, except it don't get sun much."

"I betcha Gizmos live in nice places. I betcha they got everything you could want. Fancy clothes, and mechies for servants, and shiny plastic furniture, and steel base apartments. It must be heaven," she said wistfully.

"I used to think so."

"And now you don't? Why not, Jake?"

He thought about it. Why not?

"Acob Dam didn't have none of that stuff," he began, "or want it neither. Acob just wanted the warmth of the sun on the windows of his parents' house, his books, his toys and his flute. You ever notice that little bit of flute music in the background of the show just when the story-teller starts talking? Real dim like. Nice touch, huh? None

of the alien kids shifted into creatures that used mechies or tech. All of them chose to go to peaceful places. Me, if I could, I'd choose same as them, and I miss the sun, too. I want it back, like Acob does," he finally finished.

"Oh, Jake, you ain't never had much sun to miss. Whatcha thinking about?"

"I had sun in hospital. Have it a bit in Mrs. Garvey's place, and in her books there's sun. You know, she's got more books than gizmos, ain't that something?"

"You really saying you don't want gizmos no more?" Mellie asked, her mouth open.

"I don't know what I really want no more, excepting Evan would be all right."

She didn't answer and he concentrated on moving along. It was hard work. Alvin grinned when he saw them walk up, his broad face widening further into his smile, his skin crinkling into deep lines.

"Been waiting for the two of you. Heard you were coming back today, Jake. How's it going?"

"Slow, real slow," he said.

"I think you grew while you was laid up. Must be all that rich hospital food," Alvin said with a wink.

"You think? Thanks for holding the button for us, Alvin," Jake smiled.

"Why would I stop now? Been doing it every day since you were four," he grinned. "Just like clockwork, four-and-a-half minutes late."

School was hard on him. He was late to every class, but mostly he was glad to be back and the teachers didn't say anything. Mr. Ap-pel gave him the extension on his project. He'd gotten Jake ten extra days. It wasn't much, but it was the best he'd been able to do.

"Mr. Lawrence, please stay a moment. I wanted to say, if you need any help, I'd be happy to meet you after school, or perhaps Mrs. Garvey could help you."

SHE DIDN'T ANSWER AND HE CONCENTRATED ON MOVING ALONG. IT WAS HARD WORK.
ALVIN GRINNED WHEN HE SAW THEM WALK UP, HIS BROAD FACE WIDENING FURTHER INTO
HIS SMILE. HIS SKIN CRINKLING INTO DEEP LINES.
"BEEN WAITING FOR THE TWO OF YOU. I HEARD YOU
WERE COMING BACK TODAY, JAKE. HOW'S IT GOING?
SLOW? REAL SLOW?" HE SAID.
MILLIE JUMPED IN AND PULLED JAKE UP WITH A STEADYING HAND AND THEY CROUCHED NEAR THE CAB
HOPING TO AVOID NOTICE. BUT ALVIN BLEW IT BY CALLING LOUDLY "HEY, BACK THERE. WHERE TO?"

HE'D GOTTEN JAKE TEN EXTRA DAYS. IT WASN'T MUCH BUT IT WAS THE BEST HE'D BEEN ABLE TO DO.
"MR. LAWRENCE, PLEASE STAY A MOMENT. I WANTED TO SAY, IF YOU NEED ANY HELP, I'D BE HAPP-
TO MEET YOU AFTER SCHOOL, OR PERHAPS MRS. CARVEY COULD HELP YOU."

"Aw, she don't know that much," Jake said. He wanted to see Mr. Ap-pel's response.

"That would surprise me, but ..."

"Why? She's just an old lady."

"I suppose so," he agreed reluctantly.

At the end of the day, Jake was exhausted. Mellie sat with him under the tree while everyone else left.

"This new principal, why's he after us?" Jake finally asked.

"The teachers say we got a new regional governor who hates poor folks."

"Yeah? Then he hates a whole load of people."

Mellie nodded as she helped him up.

"My pa called the school," she said with a sigh.

"What'd he want?"

"To see me. School told him I could talk to him on the phone tomorrow morning."

"You going to?"

"Guess so. School says I gotta. He's got law on his side, they say."

They stepped into the street and Mellie jerked back. Her pa was at the corner with a couple of Tattoos.

"Hey," Alvin called just then from a battered-up, old truck. "I'm collecting some supplies for the school. You two need a hitch? Jump on the back."

Mellie jumped in and pulled Jake up with a steady-ing hand. They crouched near the cab hoping to avoid no-tice, but Alvin blew it by calling loudly, "Hey, back there, where to, Jake, Mellie?"

"Sixty-fifth block, Zone D," Jake called out quickly.

"We don't live there," Mellie protested quietly. "It's in the wrong direction."

"That's right, but I want your pa to think we do. I

AT THE END OF THE DAY, JAKE WAS EXHAUSTED. NELLIE SAT WITH HIM UNDER THE TREE
WHILE EVERYONE ELSE LEFT. "THIS NEW PRINCIPAL, WHY IS HE AFTER US?" JAKE FINALLY ASKED.
"THE TEACHERS SAY WE GOT A NEW PRINCIPAL, GOVERNOR, WHO HATES POOR PEOPLE."
"YEAH, THEN HE HATES A WHOLE CATLOAD OF PEOPLE." NELLIE NODDED AS SHE HELPED HIM UP.
"I OVERHEARD HIM TELL HIM HE COULD TALK TO HIM ON THE PHONE TOMORROW MORNING.
'I GUESS SO,' SHE NODDED AS I GOTTA HAVE IT. GOTTA A X ON HIS SIDE, THEY SAY."
THEY SLIPPED INTO HIS FEET AND NELLIE EASED BACK. HER PAW WAS AT THE CORNER WITH A COUPLE OF TATTOOS.
THEY AIN'T CALLED US THEN FROM A BATTERED UP OLD TRUCK. "I'M COME TO SAVE US, PLEASE FOR THE SCHOOL.
YOU GOTTA X GO NEED AN A LITTLE SCHOOL UP AROUND THE FREE BACKS."

I AIN'T LEAVING HIM, MONK'S GURLEY AND BEGAN THE SAD NODDING AT THE TATTOOS, WHO
WERE ALREADY FAILING AT A CABBY. "YOUR PA MISTAKEN X WORKING IT AT FOLD A CABBY." JAKE
REMARKED TO HER, WATCHING THE WAS A FILE INTO THE WHITE A. UN PICKED UP SPEED A LITTLE
BUT ROCKS WERE ONLY ALLOWED ON THE YARD OR X RUTTED SIDE STREETS. HE WAITED AND TURNED
WHAT OLD BUILDING WAS SOME X LONG THE GABY. SEED ONE X OR HER AN X LOOK AT MIGHT HOSE LOG CHAP Y
KIDS PEOPLE GARDENING, TALKING TO EACH OTHER AS THEY WORKED ON THEIR YARDS."
MAYBE IT HAD BEEN NICE BUT NOW THE ROADS WERE LINED IN TRASH. THE YARD WAS
HALF DECROWNED UNDER FOR X GONE OUT MACHINE PARTS ROT HOLES OPEN ON THE STREETS
AND FILLED BACK UP WITH MUD AND DIRT. JAKE'S LEG ACHED FROM THE ROCKING.

ain't leading him to Mrs. Garvey and Evan," he said, nodding at the Tattoos who were already hailing a cabby. "Your pa musta been working to afford a cabby," Jake remarked to her, watching the men pile into the vehicle.

Alvin picked up speed a little, but trucks were only allowed on the narrow, rutted, side streets. He twisted and turned with a lot of sudden movements, sometimes losing the cabby.

"Used to be nice over here," Alvin called back to them. "Fancy houses, lots of happy kids, people gardening, talking to each other as they worked in their yards."

Maybe it had been nice, but now the roads were lined in trash. The walkways had become dumps for worn out machine parts. Pot holes opened in the streets and filled back up with mud and grit. Jake's leg ached from the bouncing.

"Almost there," Alvin called. "Funny, I didn't picture you two living over here."

The cabby was back again.

"Jake, what are we gonna do?" Mellie asked.

"I got it planned, Mellie. You gotta trust me. No matter what, promise me, you'll follow my lead. No matter what!"

He called his thanks to Alvin and popped off the truck. He swung along on his crutches as fast as he could, hoping they had a big enough lead. Another block and they would probably be safe. Mellie kept glancing back and he kept urging her forward. The cabby was in no rush. The Tattoos probably thought there was nowhere for them to go. Mellie and Jake turned the corner, and half way down the block, the road and the walkway ended at the edge of a field.

"That's the Dead Zone," Mellie gasped and stopped.

"Go, Mellie," he said, pushing at her to continue.

"Jake, we'll die for sure if we go in there."

"No, Mellie, we won't. Things live in there. I seen them. Now go."

In the light he could easily see the line marking the change to the Dead Zone that he had missed in the dark. Weeds and spiky flowers grew right up to the ragged end of the concrete. A single tendril of green was creeping its way onto the walk. Behind them the cabby had stopped and the Tattoos were piling out.

"Run, now, Mellie, go for it!" he yelled and gave her a shove.

He turned, raised a crutch up behind his head, and tossed it like a javelin thrower in one of Mrs. Garvey's books. A Tattoo went down. He shoved off with the other crutch and followed Mellie into the weeds, like a three-legged dog at a hobble.

The Tattoos had stopped, but Mellie's father bellowed after them, "I'm gonna kill you two!"

"Here's your chance, come and get us," Jake called back, challenging him.

The man stood frozen at the edge of the walk. Finally he stomped on the thin, green tendril and backed up towards the cabby.

CHAPTER 19

"You dumb kids! You just saved me the trouble of finishing you off. Have fun in there!" Mellie's pa cackled loudly. He waved with a big grin and got into the cabby.

"He's right," Mellie whispered. "We're as good as dead. Everybody knows that."

"There's grasses and weeds in here, and they're not dead, Mellie," Jake pointed out.

"Yeah, just deformed and ugly."

"Aw Mellie, just look at them weeds. They're blooming. See, they got beautiful little flowers on them," he said, picking one delicately between his fingers. "Smell good, too," he added as he sniffed it.

"Jake," she yelled. "We're in the D-E-A-D Zone. Dead, get it? Everything in here was poisoned before we was born, before the Plague, before my pa was born."

"So what? Maybe it's not poisoned no more," he yelled back. "Lots of things ain't what we been told. Lots! Listen, Mellie, it's like on 'Colony'. Those kids on that ship didn't get told everything neither. They shoulda been. It woulda been better for them. Trust me, I'll betcha we're safer in here than out on the streets. I'll betcha."

He struggled to his feet and jerked her to hers. The cabby was still waiting. Mellie's pa probably thought they'd come out. No way! He pulled her further into the field. Tears trickled down her face.

"I don't wanna die," she sobbed.

"Don't worry. We ain't gonna die, unless we go back the way we come and run into your pa. Now come on," he said.

"What are we gonna do in here?"

"We're gonna look for an address."

"In here? Why? Whose?"

"The storyteller's. He may live in here."

"Jake, no one lives here! There ain't even any build-ings in here. This is the Dead Zone. There ain't no ad-dresses in it. It's deserted, off limits!"

"You're wrong. There's an address listed in the phone book that would hafta be in here."

"So what? It's just somebody's idea of a joke is all."

"Maybe, Mellie, maybe, but then again what a great hiding place the Zone makes."

"If you wanna hide, why list an address?"

"It musta been listed a long time ago. Who knows, he mighta not been hiding then."

"Anyways, Jake, anyone who listed it in here that long ago'd be dead by now."

"Mrs. Garvey's listed and she's still alive. Somebody who'd hide in here wouldn't wanna get too popular. If he did, he might stop showing up for his DV show. Might just vanish back into hiding. No one thought his show would make it. Remember how weird it seemed, him just sitting there, telling it, no tech nor nothing? But the show made it, got popular, and now he's gone."

"You're nuts if you think the storyteller lives in here."

"We'll see. I'm going with my gut."

They walked in silence a little while, kicking at the grass. Every once in a while, Mellie sobbed.

"Mellie, I just gotta find the storyteller. I gotta find him for me, and I gotta find him for all you guys. I'm sorry about bringing you in here, Mellie, but as long as we're here, do you mind looking?"

"Harm's done already, I guess. We might as well keep going now," she said after sticking out her lip and pouting for a moment.

They lifted their feet high, to avoid the long, sharp-edged blades of grass that hid between flowering weeds, and where they stepped, the grass stayed flattened.

"I feel like Hansel and Gretel," Mellie said. " You don't think Pa'll follow us in here, do you?"

"I doubt it. Tattoos are real superstitious."

A herd of what could only be fabled bunnies bounded out of their way. "See that," Jake said triumphantly. "I told you living things was in here."

"They did lie to us," Mellie said softly, watching the bunny tails bound out of sight.

"I think they believed it themselves," Jake said.

"Why?"

"Maybe they was scared. I been trying to remember what they told us about the Dead Zone in school. You remember, Mellie?"

"No, I don't remember. Jake, let's go home now."

"Not yet."

He dragged her on. In places the land rose as if something lay buried below, then fell again. Wild blooming bushes spread across stony ground. Delicate birdsong mixed with the keening cry of a hawk that was perched in a dead tree. Small birds took flight, and the winged keener swooped down into the flock, and plucked one out in its sharp claws.

"Wow," Jake said. "See, Mellie, this place ain't dead, not by a long shot."

"Jake, there," she whispered.

Ahead of them was a startling, blackened shell of a building. The glass in its windows had all been blown out. Its stone walls screamed with the scars of fire. Around its front steps was an array of yellow flowers caught in a breeze, standing like sirens nodding at the doors.

"Musta been beautiful here once," Mellie said, watching the flowers bob.

He nodded. "What was it the storyteller said about yellow bugs? You remember, don't you, Mellie?"

"Sorta. Why?"

"Those yellow flowers, the tiny ones with black dots, look kinda like bugs, don't you think?"

"Not to me, Jake. Bugs are bugs, big, black and ugly."

He limped up to pick a flower near the top of the steps when a voice seared the air.

"Don't," it grumbled, "those are mine."

"Sorry," Jake said, looking around, not seeing anyone. "Who are you?"

"It doesn't matter. What are you doing here, boy?"

"We're looking for someone."

"No one lives here except the dead, haven't you heard?"

"You live here," Mellie said to the voice.

"Same thing. Dead."

"We're looking for a Mr. J. Adam," Jake sputtered.

"Who? Oh, that DV fellow. Why?"

"I need to talk to him."

"Too bad about that. He doesn't exist."

"Wait." But the voice was gone and the doors to the building were still dark and closed, guarding the interior.

Jake sat down.

"You were right, Jake. It ain't all dead in here," Mellie said, taking his hand.

"Mellie, whatcha think he meant when he said J. Adam didn't exist?"

"I don't know. Maybe he just ain't here."

"But how's this guy know about him?"

"Maybe he has DV, like us."

"In here?" Jake asked, shaking his head.

"Well, why not? You claim there's an address somewhere in here," she said sarcastically. "Let's go home."

"Let's go inside first," he said.

Mellie pulled back. "I wanna leave now, Jake."

"But, the voice might be him."

"No, I wanna go home."

"I'm going in, Mellie. My time is running low, and I've gotta find this J. Adam guy. If you don't wanna come with me, sit here on the steps and wait."

He limped up to the doors without waiting for her answer, but he could feel her hand holding onto his shirt. Pushing the doors open with the crutch, he slid through. High, dark ceilings hung above them covered in mosaics of blunt-toothed snakes eating their own tails. A slight breeze sifted through the dank air stirring dust, bringing with it a distant, sudden scent of flowers. A narrow stair-well wound upwards. Holding to a wall for support, Jake ascended the stairs, Mellie still hanging onto his shirt tail.

The stairs ended, leaving them standing on heavy stone floors. Shafts of sunlight lanced through tall, thin windows, and cross-currents of air sent their hair flying. The hallway was circular, the interior walls lined with glass cases, which in turn were filled with stone carvings, and books, and shiny jewelry. Mellie released his shirt and they pressed their noses against the cases reading the titles of books: *The Odyssey, Tales of the Brothers Grimm, Jo's Boys, Tennyson's Poetical Works, To Kill a Mockingbird, The Autobiography of Malcolm X, Cry the Beloved Country, The Just So Stories, The Canterbury Tales, Babar, To the Light-house, Walden, The Ramayana, The Scarlet Letter, Robin Hood, Crime and Punishment.*

"You ever heard of any of these?" he asked Mellie.

"Actually, I mighta seen a few at Mrs. Garvey's with the same titles. There are so many here. They go all the way around this floor."

"Yeah, they do. Whatcha think of these statues?" he asked, scratching at his head.

I'm going in Millie. My time is running low and I've got a find it his J. Adam guy. If you don't want to come with me, sit here on the steps and wait." He limped out the doors without waiting for her answer, but he could tell her hand had dragging on to his shirt. Pushing the doors open with the crutch he slid through. High dark ceiling hung above them covered in mosaics of blunt toothed snakes eating their own tails. A slight breeze sifted through

through the dark air, stirring dust, bringing with it a distant, sudden scent of flowers. A narrow stairwell wound upward. Holding to a wall for support, Jake ascended the stairs, Millie still hanging on to his shirt tail. The stairs ended leaving them standing on heavy stone floors. Shafts of sunlight lanced through tall, thin windows and caused currents of air to set their hair flying. The hallway was circular, the interior walls lined with glass cases which in turn were filled with stone carvings, and books,

"Got me. I'm gonna follow the books for a while," Mellie said, meandering on along the curve.

He sat in a shaft of sunlight and stared at a carved figure whose painted eyes gazed back at him. He knew he was being watched, and not by a sculpture. He could feel it up and down his spine.

"Something, huh, Mellie?" he called to her.

"Yeah, something. Over here are some authors I heard of: Rankoni, Plithe, Marvine. Mrs. Garvey would love this," her voice came back to him.

"Eloise Garvey?" a growling voice asked, as Mellie rounded the circle and Jake jumped up at the sound.

Jake forgot his foot and would have gone down almost as fast as he had jumped up, but hands caught him.

"Now you've just had to come in here and find me, haven't you?" the voice belonging to the hands asked.

"You are J. Adam, the storyteller, ain't you?" Jake asked as the hands held him, preventing him from turning.

"I quit being him so I wouldn't have nosy people poking into my business," came the answer.

"You quit? You weren't canned?" Mellie asked.

"Quite right. I quit. I only began telling the story out of a momentary fit of loneliness. Who would have thought anyone would care about my tale? But people did, and they got curious. They started waiting outside the studio for me. They tried to get my autograph. They snapped my photo. Even my cantankerous tech man wanted to know more about me. He actually asked me to go out drinking with him. So I quit, and vanished."

"But, you really are him?" Mellie asked, a tone of delight creeping into her voice.

"Who?"

"The storyteller, J. Adam."

"Not really. Now, how is Eloise?"

HE SAT IN A SHAFT OF SUNLIGHT AND STARED AT A CARVED FIGURE WHOSE PAINTED EYES GAZED BACK AT HIM. HE KNEW HE WAS BEING WATCHED, AND NOT BY A SCULPTURE. HE COULD FEEL IT UP AND DOWN HIS SPINE

'SOMETHING, HUH... MILLIE?' HE CALLED TO HER

'YEAH, SOMETHING... OOH! HERE ARE SOME AUTHORS I HEARD OF. RANK ON, RUTH E. MARINE, MRS. CARLEY... WOULD I LIKE THESE?' HER VOICE CAME BACK TO HIM

'HELLO? ARE CAROL HERE?' A CROWN OVER NOISE ASKED AS MILLIE FOUND THE FLOOR CLUE AND JAKE UMBLED UP AT THE SECOND

JAKE FORGOT ABOUT HIS FOOT AND WOULD HAVE GONE DOWN ALMOST AS FAST AS HE HAD UMBLED UP, BUT HAND CAUGHT HIM

'YOU WOULDN'T BE IN A SHADY DOORWAY IN HERE AND FIND ME, HAVEN'T YOU?' THE VOICE BEHIND HOLDING TO HIS HANDS ASKED

'YOU ARE... I AM, THE STORYTELLER, AREN'T YOU?' JAKE ASKED AS THE HAND SHELD HIM

'I QUIT BEING HIM, SO I WOULDN'T HAVE NO PEOPLE OR NO NO NO BLUENESS.' GAVE THE ANSWER

'YOU QUIT? YOU WEREN'T CANNED?' MILLIE ASKED

'QUITE. I QUIT. ONLY BEGAN TELLING THE STORY, QUIT OF A MOMENTARY FIT OF
LONELINESS. WHO WOULD HAVE THOUGHT ANYONE WOULD CARE ABOUT MY TALE
BUT PEOPLE DID. AND THEY GOT CURIOUS. THEY STARTED WAITING OUTSIDE THE STUDIO
FOR ME. THEY TRIED TO GET IN MY AUTOGRAPH. THEY WAITED. MY CHOICE IN THE CURTAIN FOR OLD
TECH. WHO WANTED TO KNOW MORE ABOUT ME. HE ACTUALLY ASKED ME TO CO OUT DRINKING WITH

HIM. SO I QUIT. AND VANISHED.

"Mrs. Garvey? You know her?" Jake asked warily.

"Yes, how is she?"

"She's fine. If you know her, how come she's never recognized you on the DV?" Jake asked.

"She watches? Well, she would hardly have recognized me with the makeup I wore on the DV show. Who are you two, anyway?" the storyteller asked.

"I'm Jake Lawrence and this is Mellie. Mrs. Garvey takes care of us and my little brother, Evan. Why don't you come out of the shadows and talk to us?" Jake said, twisting his head.

"Why should I?"

The hands released him, leaving him gently balanced on his feet.

"I gotta interview you or get kicked outta school," Jake spat out quickly. "Please talk to me."

He turned, but saw no one. "Why do you live in the Dead Zone, and why do you say you're not J. Adam? I know you're him."

"He's hidden in that really dark corner," Mellie whispered. "I sorta saw his shadow slide in there."

"I will not answer any of your questions. I do not wish to be interviewed nor to be on DV ever again," the voice answered after a drawn-out pause.

"Oh, come on, how can it hurt? Besides, you gotta go back on DV. Please! People think the DV station fired you. They're angry. You gotta at least go on and say good-bye," Jake pleaded.

"I can't. I won't. Too many questions have already arisen. Too many people know about me. I should never have drawn all that attention to myself. Now tell me about Eloise."

"No way," Jake said. "You want info, you give info.

Rule of the streets. You ain't even come out of the shadows. I ain't giving out nothing about Mrs. Garvey to some guy I can't even see."

"Ah, I see and I do understand. We're at a stalemate here," the voice mumbled.

"You betcha," Jake said. "Whatcha gonna do?"

"You're gonna trust each other," Mellie said softly. "Listen, Mr. Adam, if that's who you are, Jake's a good guy. He's tough, but he keeps his word. If he says he'll keep your secrets, he will. As for Mrs. Garvey, she loves him like a son."

"Is that so, young lady?"

"Yes, it is, and Jake loves her and Evan and maybe, even me. Jake loves real easy. And Jake," she said turning to him, "you don't got much choice. You gotta take this chance. You already took so many to get this far."

"Is that so?" Jake murmured like an echo. "Okay, Mellie, if you say so."

Someone stepped from the shadows into the light. He was slender, his skin translucent, pulled smoothly over high cheekbones and a heavy brow. The eyes were golden brown, the hair a fuzz of blonde. His hands were jammed into deep pockets. He held himself tightly, neither young nor old, his age indefinable.

"You ain't him," Jake said.

"No? Well, I told you that, but actually, it is just that I do not appear to be him. Now what of Eloise?"

"I said, you ain't him."

"I am. I told you, I am just not camera-ready, makeup and all that. Believe me, I am, unfortunately, the soul you call J. Adam. Please, tell me of Eloise."

There was something so plaintive and sad in the voice that Jake relented.

"Whatcha wanna know?"

"Is she happy?"

"That ain't much to ask, but before I answer, who are you?"

"Did she have children? How old is she?"

"What business of yours is that?"

"I just want to know if she's happy. Is that too much to ask?"

"I ain't telling you no more," Jake said stubbornly. "You ask and ask, but don't answer nothing."

"She's a grandmotherly age," Mellie interjected unexpectedly. "Her hair is silver, her teeth a fine white and she has wrinkles, but her eyes dance and dance."

Jake stared at Mellie. He had never noticed Mrs. Garvey's eyes.

"Ah, a lovely description," the man sighed. "And is she happy?"

"We can't tell you that," Jake said. "We don't know. Why don't you ask her yourself? We'll bring her, show her the bunnies, and the flowers, and the tower, and introduce you to her."

"Oh no, my dear children. No, no."

"Why not?" Jake asked.

"Just don't bring her here! In fact, don't bring anyone else here. Enough is enough."

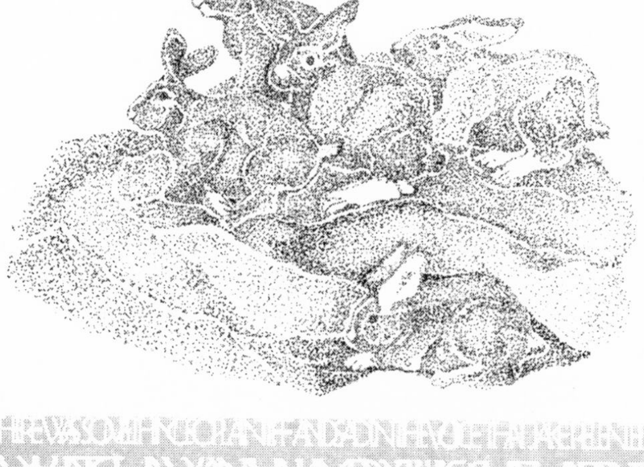

CHAPTER 20

They followed him up another flight of stairs onto a roof. From here the Dead Zone lay open to them. Flights of birds rose to the skies, flowering trees nodded and swayed.

"Why do they call it a Dead Zone?" Jake wondered aloud, shaking his head.

"It once was," J. Adam replied. "Mankind poisoned it until they had no choice but to abandon it. They thought the land was unredeemable, but nature tricked them, played possum and then reclaimed the ground, the animals, the plants. She holds them tight and dear to herself. She buried the dead machinery, the deadly chemicals under layer after layer of dirt and weeds. The toxins washed out, and behold, life."

"It's beautiful here. Find any yellow bugs?" Jake asked, surprising himself.

The storyteller smiled wistfully and shook his head. "Now, now, you mustn't get so involved with what is merely the meandering of an old man into storytelling."

"Right! Are you gonna go back on DV?" Jake asked.

"I told you, no, nor will I be interviewed."

"Then my goose is cooked. My school is gonna expel me."

"Why?"

"We got some new policies and if a student don't turn in his assignments, then they use it as an excuse to kick him out. Unfortunately for me, my assignment's to interview you."

The storyteller shook his head slowly. His hands were still deep in his pockets.

"Would your teacher be satisfied with some more stories? You could write them down as proof of an interview."

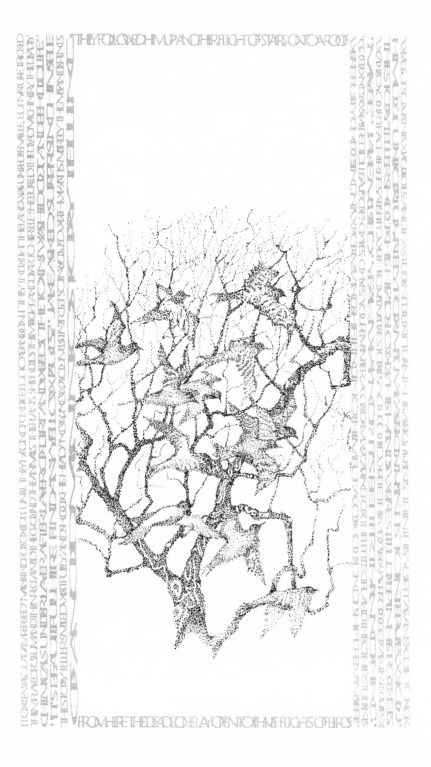

THEY FOLLOWED HIM UP AN OTHER FLIGHT OF STAIRS ONTO A ROOF

FROM HERE THE DELAYED COTE LAY OPEN TO THE FLIGHTS OF BIRDS

"Maybe," Jake mused. "Yeah, why not? It's better than nothing."

"Good. Now where did I leave off? Oh yes, oh yes. You remember, Acob Dam was caring for the little girl and the other students were busily choosing new forms and shifting into them, but Acob could not shift. Remember?"

"Right," Mellie confirmed. "How does that shifting work, anyways?"

"The trick was to be able to hold an exact, focused image in their minds as they shifted. They could shift into any stage of development they chose. Baby, adult, child, male, female, any organism that they could visualize in precise detail. Acob Dam could not do this. He was genetically defective. He could only assume the form of an already existing, living being, and that was unacceptable to him and to his people. One of the rules of Colony was to merge unobserved, and without consequences to the host beings. Acob's predicament violated this completely. If he shifted into another living being's form, he would also have to take on their memories, and in order to survive, need to take their place in the world with all that that implied. He could not do that."

"You have surely imagined your story in fine detail," Mellie remarked.

"What else have I had to do all these years in this place?"

"So what happened?" Mellie asked.

Nothing for the moment. The masters had many obligations. Two hundred children had had to be placed like orphans looking for adoptive parents. One hundred and fifty were gone, but fifty remained. They came first.

Acob Dam wandered the ship, watching his friends depart.

"Will they remember me at all?" he asked.

"No, not at all, unless you appear during the first few hours after they shift and imprint on them. After that, they are who they have become. And, if by some chance, they should remember you, it would be as if in an irritating, reoccurring dream or as a shadow."

"Then my friends no longer exist."

"They are someone else's friends now," the master said.

"Why? Why didn't we just stay at home?"

"We have told you over and over! It was too crowded. And we have evidence that those from Colony who shift achieve great things for the beings they join. It is the perfect solution."

"Except for me. What will you do with me now?" Acob asked.

"We are searching for an answer and when we have one, we will tell you."

All this time, Acob had only the child to love. He could not bear to be with the others, for they had hope. They laughed, and joked, and speculated on the future. Acob could see that neither he nor the sweet child had a future.

One day a group of thirty left. The world below was covered in soft grasses and yellow flowers. The lives they went to join were small, green humanoids, with white-feathered bodies and sharply clawed fingers. They built grass woven buildings that became dew covered in the mornings, glistening with moisture. The climate was never cold. There were no predators. They bred easily, prolifically, joyfully. Thirty little green people left the ship for what looked like a paradise.

"Might have only looked like a Paradise and been something else, like a backwards Dead Zone," Jake commented to the storyteller.

"There was always a risk," J. Adam said.

Jake looked up as the sun vanished behind thick thunderheads that were blackening the air.

"We gotta go home. It's gonna storm bloody murder," Jake announced, "but we'll be back, I promise."

"Fine, but bring no one with you, or I shall vanish completely," the storyteller reminded them.

"Okay, okay," Jake said. "But, when we come back, I got questions in bunches."

"Go now, before the storm hits and, Jake, not too many questions," the storyteller smiled sadly.

When they got down to the ground they looked up at the roof line. The storyteller waved a large hand at them, his thin body glowing whitely against the dark sky.

"Come on Mellie. I'm sure your pa will be gone with this storm coming up."

She ran ahead of his hobbling gait, wind whipping her hair, making her pants flap against her legs. Lightning split through the clouds, but the rain held off until they reached the edge of the Dead Zone. If the cabby was still there it was invisible in the downpour. The deluge hit metal roofs like it was banging a drum, and water rose quickly to their ankles. He kept his sore foot raised, but even with the crutch, he slipped over and over.

They clung to each other and finally fell into a deep door frame, huddling there, thin body to thin body. The rain reached into their hiding place and lashed them with its icy sting. Jake tried the door, but it didn't give. All these buildings were storehouses, locked and keyed.

"Jake," Mellie screamed above the drumming. "How we gonna get home?"

"We're lucky. When this kinda rain ends they send out assayer trucks to check the damage. We'll jump a ride."

"Can you with your foot?"

"I'll have to," he said.

They waited, wet and shivering until the rain turned to drizzle, and finally stopped. They waited again for the trucks, whose little yellow head-lamps looked like the warmest things Jake had ever seen.

CHAPTER 21

As Mrs. Garvey flung the door open, her expression of fear relaxed into relief.

"Good lord, you two had me worried sick. Don't stand in the hall. Come in, right now. Drip on that rug a minute and I'll get towels," she said almost imperiously in her distress. She fussed over them until they were in dry clothes and she had filled them with hot milk and toast.

"Where were you? Don't you know not to get caught in that kind of rain?"

"Mellie's pa chased us. We had to hide a long time."

"I told you he would be trouble," Mrs. Garvey said.

"Mrs. Garvey," Jake said, stopping her, "how come folks know your name?"

"Who knows me?"

"Lots of people. The school nurse, for one. Are you a doc or not?"

She sighed. "A long time ago, I practiced a bit. It was nothing to brag about, and I don't like to tell anyone."

"But, you could be rich," Jake pointed out.

"Not really. They don't use real doctors much now, Jake. People blamed doctors for the Plague. They lost faith in them, even hated them. Nobody wanted to be responsible for the Plague. Nobody even wanted to admit there was a plague, but if there was one they convinced themselves it was the doctors' faults."

"How could they deny the Plague. People were dying all over the place, weren't they?" Mellie asked.

"Yes, of course," Mrs. Garvey said.

"So, who was really responsible for the Plague?" Jake asked.

"No one ever owned up to it. Maybe it was just nature getting her revenge, maybe it was gene manipulators, or biological warfare or bad judgment, or escaped lab viruses or ... The list was endless," Mrs. Garvey sighed. "At first people were asymptomatic. When they did get sick they didn't realize they all had the same disease. You see, everyone had different symptoms and everyone had a different notion about what was wrong with them. I was young when it struck and new to the medical profession. I began to see a pattern to the illness. Five years later, I proved the pattern. By then it was too late for a lot of people, especially those in the final stages when convulsions and fevers took over and ravaged the victims. Young, old, male, female, children and babies, it didn't much matter, they all died." She stared blankly into space for a moment.

"But you got famous, didn't you?" Mellie asked very gently.

"Famous or infamous, who knows. What I discovered panicked everyone, even though it eventually led to a vaccine. Sometimes I think people would rather have died not knowing the truth. My husband and I were driven behind these very walls to raise our son. I waited for it all to fade, and it did, as scientists found the way to vaccinate uninfected people. But, for lots of families, it was too late."

Jake wondered why he wasn't Plague-defective and Evan was?

"When my son found out he'd been affected by the Plague, he ran away. I was never sure how it had happened. I never found out if he was born with it or not. I had always known there was something different about him. He was seventeen and had a girl friend. She was a lovely, young Gizmo girl. They wanted to raise a family together, and when they went to be examined for the pre-marital medical, they found an unknown, mutated gene in him. It was one of the symptoms of the Plague. He blamed me. He said I had exposed myself and him by doing research. He screamed at me that I was not only losing my child, but that I would never have grandchildren. He was so young, so unforgiving." Her eyes filled with tears. "Then Ted died and I was alone, all alone."

"Not anymore. You got us now, Mrs. Garvey," Jake said gently.

"Yes, the three of you. Now you two get to bed. School comes up fast and early tomorrow." She blew her nose loudly into a handkerchief.

School did come early and the day dragged by. Jake spent most of it thinking about Evan. The little boy seemed weaker. He rarely raised his head up straight and something seemed lost in his eyes. Maybe it had never been there. Maybe Jake was just seeing Evan differently. Sure, he had always claimed Evan knew a lot more than people thought, but maybe it truly had been wishful thinking. He tried to remember if Evan had always drooled this much, but couldn't.

How could Evan have been born Plague-stricken, and Jake have been born normal? Why couldn't Evan speak? Mrs. Garvey should know. He was going to make her give him a straight and true answer.

Evan greeted him at the door in the afternoon. Jake gave him a hug, but this time the boy's arms hung limply at his sides. Jake planted a kiss on his face and Evan's hands clenched and unclenched, clenched and unclenched reflexively, over and over.

"Oh, Evan!" he whispered.

Mrs. Garvey was standing just behind the child.

"Hi," Jake said.

"Hi, Jake."

"What's happening to him, Mrs. Garvey? Tell me true," he begged.

"Come on. Let's make tea." She took Evan's hand, pulled him to an overstuffed chair, and plucked him into it.

She gave Jake a cup and toast with jam before she said, "Evan is deteriorating, getting worse rapidly, now."

"I thought so."

"It happens to Plague victims. At first I thought he was born with the Plague, the result of a prenatal exposure, but now I think not. I think Evan was deformed in some other way when he was born, and so your mother never bothered to get him vaccinated."

"You mean he didn't hafta be like this?"

"Maybe not. He probably would never have been like other kids, but I don't think he had to contract the Plague."

"Oh, Ma," he groaned. "How come you did this to Evan?"

"Jake, I'm sure she thought he was already infected. Most people still think any defect they or their children have is due to the Plague. My own son believed that. I never found out if it was true or not for him. He never gave me the chance. It was one of the many Plague myths."

"Can't you cure Evan? You're a doc."

"I wish I could, but all I can do is make him comfortable until it's over."

"You won't be around forever, Mrs. Garvey."

"No, Jake, I won't at my age, but I'll be around long enough for Evan."

She was saying Evan was going to die and soon. She was saying there wasn't any hope.

"No," he screamed. "He ain't gonna die. I won't let him. He's all I got!"

"Jake, oh Jake, I know it hurts," she said, reaching to him, but he shook her off.

"I hate Ma! I used to think she was good, all soapy and warm, and that it was men what turned her bad.

Now I know she was always rotten, just stinking rotten all the way through and through," he said, his voice trailing off into tears.

"I'm sure she didn't understand what she had done."

He slammed his fist into a wall. "How long?" he finally stammered.

"I don't know. No one does. He could get better for a time, or it could be very fast. We'll just have to love him until it's over."

"It's not fair," he sobbed and limped out of the apartment, down to the street. He hurried around the corner, heard Mrs. Garvey calling after him, heard Mellie join her, their voices straining to bring him back. He ignored them.

Evan couldn't die! He wouldn't let him. It wasn't fair. He was only a little boy.

Jake hobbled on, weaving in and out of streets to be sure no one followed him. He jumped a slow moving van on a rutted street until he made his way back to the Zone.

He stumbled into it, realizing he was being drawn to the storyteller like an iron filing to a magnet. Why? What could the storyteller offer him? Maybe he could hide with the old man, maybe he could be safe, too.

The yellow flowers nodded at him. One drop of red sat on a yellow petal like a bright call of blood. At a closer look, it was a perfect, round dot of a beetle, spotted with black. A tear landed next to it, and the drop of blood flew off.

"Mr. Adam, where are you?" Jake called. "Please, can I talk to you? Please, please be here. I need you," he called, but nobody answered.

He sat on the steps and let the sun seep into him until he felt thick and syrupy, and fell asleep. Dew covered him before he awoke to fingers on his shoulder.

"What are you doing here, Jake?" Mr. Adam asked.

"There wasn't nowhere else to come. Evan is dying! Mrs. Garvey says Evan is gonna die real soon."

"We all die, Jake," the storyteller said.

"But he's so young! I wish he could shift to be someone or something else. A poof and a snap, and he'd be whole."

"But he can't," the storyteller pointed out.

"No, but if he could poof, click, and he'd be healthy! Alive! Magic!"

"Jake, I carefully plotted everything in 'Colony' that seems like magic to you. I made up shifting as part of the aliens' biological makeup. It's only make-believe, a fantasy I made up in my loneliness to keep myself company."

"I know! I know there ain't nobody that can really shift. I know it's only a story, but I can still wish it was true. I want Evan to live so badly."

"Remember the little girl in the story? She wasn't supposed to live either. She was born at the wrong time, just as Evan was.

"But did Acob's little girl die?"

"Wait," the storyteller said gently. "I'll tell you next time you come. Now, you need to go home."

"No, and I ain't going back to school, neither."

"Jake, Mrs. Garvey must understand how you feel. She lost her son, remember? He was a boy a little older than you, wasn't he? You told me she loves Evan. Don't you think it hurts her? She needs you and you need her."

"Maybe she's wrong. She's gotta be wrong."

"Perhaps, but she may be right, too. It isn't her fault, you know."

"No, I guess not," Jake said, tears dripping down his nose and cheeks.

Gentle hands caught him from behind and turned him. Mrs. Garvey drew him against her.

"Jake, please come home," she said.

"How'd you get here?"

"Mellie brought me. Please, Jake, come home now."

"Okay, I'm ready, I guess."

He looked around, but Mr. Adam had disappeared.

"Mrs. Garvey paid a lot to get a cabby to wait at the edge of the Zone for us, so we gotta hurry," Mellie said.

She was carrying Evan, his head lolling in sleep on her shoulder.

"Yeah, sure, let's go," he said, taking Evan from her.

He held the warm body tightly, trying hard to will the boy to be well. Mrs. Garvey touched his shoulder.

"Are you all right, Jake? I'm truly sorry I can't help Evan."

"Me too, Mrs. Garvey, but I know it ain't your fault."

He had never been in a cabby before. They were crowded into the back and at every bump, Jake banged his head against the ceiling. It was shabby inside, even though cabby drivers waxed and waxed, and polished and polished the outsides until people could see a distorted version of themselves in the finish of any parked cabby.

The driver was quiet at first, but finally couldn't hold in his curiosity.

"You all went into the Dead Zone and walked back out?" the driver asked.

"Yes," Mrs. Garvey said calmly.

"Don't usually wait, even if someone pays me, but I hadda find out what happened to you."

Jake's street wits told him to take the conversation in another direction.

"Whadya do in there?" the man persisted.

"Barely got out alive," Jake said, cutting Mrs. Garvey off before she could reply.

ONE HAND CAUGHT HIM AROUND THE HAND TURNED HIM AWAY. "I'M AGAINST A CUTTER," SAID MRS. CARVEY SAID. "JAKE HE'LL BE COMFORTABLE...

"HOW DID YOU GET THERE?"

"MILLIE BROUGHT ME. PLEASE JAKE. COME SHOW ME NOW."

"OKAY I'M READY I GUESS." HE LOOKED AROUND BUT MR. ADAM HAD DISAPPEARED.

"MRS. CARVEY PAID A LOT TO GET JAKE BY TO WAIT AT THE CURB OF THE ZONE FOR US. SO HURRY UP," MILLIE SAID.

SHE WAS CARRYING EVAN HIS HEAD LOLLING IN SLEEP ON HER SHOULDER.

"YEAH, IT'S URE. LET'S GO," HE SAID TAKING EVAN FROM HER. HE HELD THE WARM BODY TIGHTLY TRYING HARD TO WILL

HIM TO LIVE. MRS. CARVEY TOUCHED HER HIS SHOULDER.

"ARE YOU ALL RIGHT, JAKE? I'M TRULY SORRY I CAN'T HELP EVAN."

"IT'S TOO LATE, MRS. CARVEY, BUT I FIND EXPLAINTLY YOU'D REALLY..."

HE HELD EVAN IN A CAB BY BEFORE THE CAB WAS BE CROWDED INTO THE BACK AND AT EVERY STUMP JAKE BANGED HIS HEAD

AGAINST THE CEILING. IT WAS HER AND HE BUMPED GRAY CRUSTS YARD AND YARD AND POSHED AND PUSHED HIS OUTSIDES WILL HIGH THE CLUB DE ACAR ACHED

VERSION OF THEMSELVES IN THE FINISH-UP ANY CAB BY PARKED ON THE STREET.

THE DRIVER WAS QUIET AT FIRST BUT FINALLY COULDN'T HOLD IN HIS CURIOSITY.

"YOU JALL WENT INTO THE DEAD ZONE AND WALKED BACK OUT?" THE DRIVER ASKED.

"YES," MRS. CARVEY SAID CALMLY.

JAKE'S STREET WAS TOLD HIM TO TAKE THE CONVERSATION IN ANOTHER DIRECTION.

"WHY'D YA GO IN THERE?" THE MAN PERSISTED.

"BARELY GOT YOU ALIVE," JAKE SAID CUTTING MRS. CARVEY OFF BEFORE SHE COULD REPLY.

"WHAT JAKE...?" SHE BEGAN.

"I'M SORRY MRS. CARVEY I SHOULDN'T OF TAKEN THE DARE. BUT YOU KNOW HOW THAT MAKE CAN LIE. HE'LL CRAZY.

I COULDN'T TAKE IT OR...

"Why, Jake ...," she began.

"I'm sorry, Mrs. Garvey. I shouldn't of taken the dare, but you know how that Mikel can be, real crazy, and I couldn't back down."

"You should have listened to me," she said, suddenly playing along with his lead.

"Yeah, but you shouldn't of chanced coming after me," he said.

"I couldn't leave you there. You should have known that." She even sounded angry now.

"Bad in there, huh?" the driver finally got in.

"Bad? It's the Dead Zone! And for good reason."

"Sshhhh," Mellie said, helping out with the deception. "You're gonna wake Evan."

They were quiet again. Jake wished they could have awakened Evan, but he doubted it.

The cabby man kept sneaking looks at them in his rear view mirror, staring at Jake. Jake hoped it was too dark for him to see them clearly, and bowed his head.

The cabby left them off a couple of blocks from their door, and Jake watched warily until they keyed the lock to the apartment behind them. They tucked Evan in and went to the kitchen for warm, sweet tea and crackers. Mellie kissed them goodnight, and Mrs. Garvey sipped quietly across from him. He waited for her to say something. Ma would have taken his head off by now. Actually, Ma wouldn't have come after him at all.

At last Mrs. Garvey cleared her throat.

"Who was that man you were speaking to when we first came? He looked vaguely familiar."

He answered with relief, glad she wasn't mad. "He's J. Adam, the storyteller on 'Colony'. I found him!"

"Oh!" she said. "Of course, that's it. I didn't get a very close look, but I knew he looked familiar. I just couldn't quite place him. I'm so happy for you. Is he giving you an interview?"

"Not exactly. He don't want to be interviewed. He ain't gonna answer no questions, but he's gonna tell me the rest of the story, which is even better. Mrs. Garvey, why do you think he lives there?"

"To be alone, I suppose."

"You ever met him face to face?"

"I certainly don't think so. Why, Jake?"

"He was very interested in Eloise Garvey."

"Really? Oh my, perhaps I treated him once and don't remember. Recently my memory seems to have holes and shadows in it. But, I do know I have one thing in common with him. I want anonymity, to be unrecognizable, and to be left alone."

"Sorry," Jake said. "I guess, we're putting you in a spotlight, huh?"

"I'm sorry I said that, Jake. I love you guys and that means more than anything to me. The three of you are worth taking risks for. I'll survive."

"I wish Evan would."

"Yes, so do I, Jake. Maybe our wishes will come true. You never know for sure."

She got up and left him quietly. He turned out the lights and listened to the shouts that always filtered from the street into the apartment at night.

"Naw," he said to himself, "they won't come true. Not in this place."

Wishes were never more than cracked slivers of life if you were a Streetie.

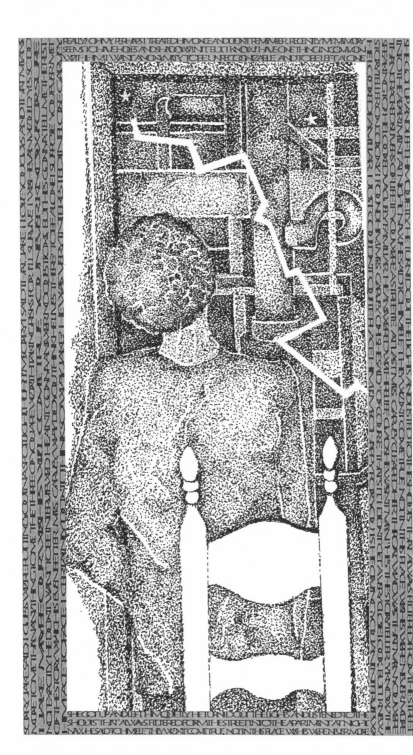

CHAPTER 22

School came. He found himself doodling cartoon versions of the storyteller in his notebook. They were bad, really bad. Head all cockeyed, huge hands, too thin body.

"Well," Mr. Ap-pel said, "are you becoming a cartoonist for a space opera?"

"No sir, I don't think so. I'm just a rotten artist," Jake smiled.

Mr. Ap-pel smiled back.

The school day ended. He and Mellie went straight to the Zone. He no longer thought of it as Dead, just the Zone. He pondered on that. It was more alive than the streets were, except it didn't have people in it.

They tried now not to trample the grass. They no longer needed to have a trail back and they didn't want any nosy cabby-men tracking them.

The blackened tower reigned over some new purple flowers which, despite three-foot stems, were dwarfed by the massive stone.

Mellie bent to sniff. Her hair had grown wild. Curly black against black stone, it vanished, making her hands a flash of light as they lifted the blossoms.

"Welcome back," the storyteller greeted them.

"We've come to listen," Mellie said.

"Good. How is Evan?"

"Home," Jake said.

They sat on cold stone on the roof.

"Now, let me think. Oh yes, we are there in the story." He began again.

One day Acob went to the library to look for books for the little girl, but they had not expected small children on the journey. Instead of finding her books, he found books for himself, which opened doors, which led to questions. At first he watched

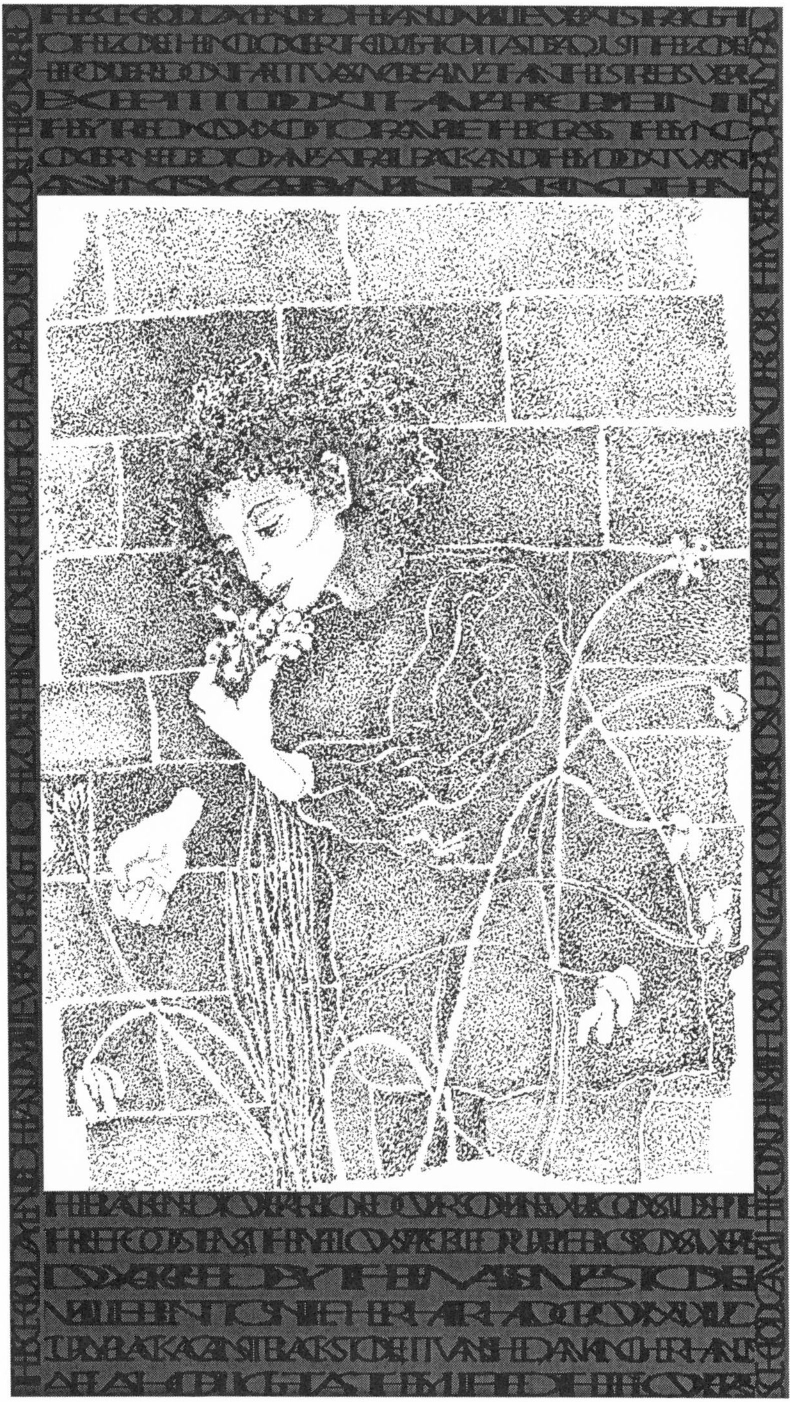

the books on screen, but his eye was drawn to the few hand-held volumes that he could take back to his room and lie quietly and read. In the end, he had too many questions.

Acob chose a time to challenge the masters when few students were left.

He entered their quarters, but did not see them. "Hello?" he called softly. There was no response. "I want answers," he said.

A master slid through a doorway, standing tall and stern over Acob. "If you have questions, come to class."

"I don't belong there and neither do my questions."

"What then? Tell me, and if your questions warrant it, I will give answers."

"What will the masters do when we are all gone? You use that phrase a lot, 'when we are gone.' But, what happens to you? Is your job over? Do you go home?"

"We keep telling you, Acob, we do not go home. The ship's power source is already near its limit, and soon we will have to find a place to colonize ourselves."

"You never go home?"

"Acob, can't you take no for an answer? We simply go on until we have no choice but to stop, find a place for ourselves and shift. If it was possible we wouldn't. Who wouldn't want the adventure to go on forever? "

"I would have chosen for it never to have begun!"

The master shook his head. "Yes, Acob, clearly you would have, and I suppose we owe you a real explanation. At home, we were elders of a celibate sect who did not believe in making the final shift. Our order had always resisted shifting. We had been ridiculed and reviled for years, and yet people had still joined us. Then Colony began and our order found its place. First we took on preparation, then exploration, and finally the actual journey and act of Colony. Without us, their could have been no Colony," the master said proudly. "We became the safety valve for our world. Soon we will shift, but it has been worth it!"

"If the child and I stay on the ship with you until the end, perhaps she will be old enough to colonize with all of us."

"No, no. You cannot stay with us. You need special accommodations, Acob. We must find a home for you now, before it is too late.. There is little enough time as it is."

"How will you find a place for me? I cannot assimilate."

"It will be a home where you will not be too noticeable."

"And the child?"

"She will have to stay with us."

"Alone, with you? Will she survive?"

"It is improbable that we will be able to wait to colonize until she is ready to shift. We did not count on placing you separately, and that has further decreased our own time to find a place to change. In any case, it would not have been enough time for her. All we can do is make her as happy as we can, as long as we can."

Acob left. He looked at the girl and felt his love well up for her. He took her by the hand, wandering and musing. There had to be a way to save her. For days, nightmares were his only dreams. He had been given few choices, but she had even fewer.

He wandered some more, wondering why everything seemed to have unexpected consequences. If Timiial had still been there, she might have understood.

The last students shifted, became gossamer-winged insects, with long waving tentacles and thin orange legs, each with sixteen, knobby joints. Their cities, suspended above vast valleys of flowers, were connected by twine-thin, silver bridges, the conical forms of their homes approachable only by flight. They spent hours cultivating and pollinating flowers, and driving off invaders who nibbled at blossoms and leaves. If a bigger animal wandered into their farms, they attacked with stingers, then flew back to their cities singing beautiful songs. The bodies they left behind decayed and enriched the soil. A few less developed animals were watched eagerly, even nurtured by the gossamer beings.

Acob watched the Colony join their winged peers, but no longer felt regret. No matter how beautiful or idyllic the beings the students had shifted into, he had no interest in joining them. He wondered if it was because he was defective, but thought it was

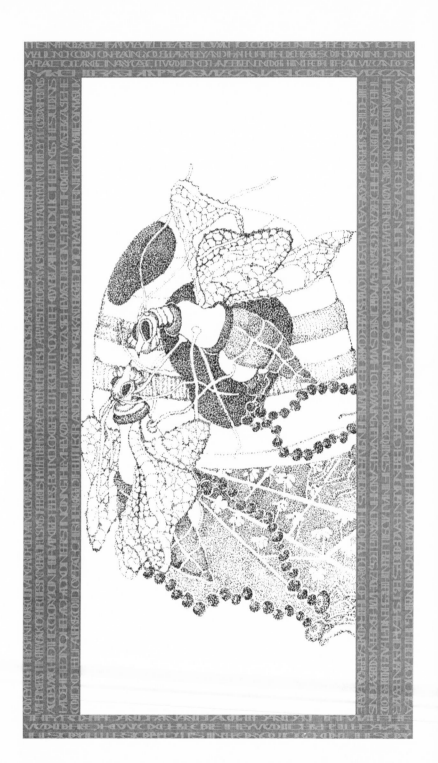

because he could not tell if the aliens could love each other. He hugged the little girl, and she hugged him back and begged him to play with her in the cold, white gymnasium.

They romped and ran and laughed, and all the while he wondered, how long before they would be pulled apart.

The storyteller stopped. "It's time for you to go home. The story is a bit longer, but go home now. Come back again, and we'll finish."

"When you finish, you gonna begin another story?" Mellie asked.

"If I have another to tell," was the answer, so softly said it sounded like a wisp of wind.

CHAPTER 23

"There was a riot," Mrs. Garvey exclaimed when they got home, "at a school in Zone A. They must have put new administrators into all the schools. At this school, the new principal tried to expel the whole student body. He claimed the students didn't learn enough to warrant the expense of school. He locked the gates and posted a notice this morning. The kids rioted. They threw stones, tore down the guard's gate, and stormed the school. It's all over the DV."

"Wow," Mellie said, sinking into a chair, eyes instantly glued to the screen.

Evan crawled over to her and pulled up like a little baby. She reached down absently and plucked him into her lap. He looked smaller, more shrunken to Jake.

Well, Ma, no more wishful thinking, no more dreaming. Evan is really drying up. He may just blow away, he heard himself say clearly, but no words came out.

The DV caught his eye now. Streeties had joined the students. Cops were strong-arming through the crowds, swinging blunt edges at legs and arms, even a few heads. Over the pictures, over the announcers' voices, a chant, a deep and throaty roar was rising.

"What are they screaming?" Mellie asked.

"They're chanting, 'School, school, school, school' over and over," Mrs. Garvey said quietly.

"Who'd have thought it?" Jake said. "Kids actually willing to fight to get into a school!"

"Yes, who would have thought it?"

At midnight the DV went off. Jake stayed up a little while. Dim starlight crept around the room like a stray cat trying to find a place to rest. Jake rubbed at his eyes and curled up in a chair to awaken only when Mrs. Garvey came to do what she called her "morning dithering" in the kitchen. He washed while lovely smells of chocolate and fresh coffee stole through the apartment. When he sat down to breakfast, he saw that Mrs. Garvey was dressed in a tidy white skirt and jacket, hair pulled into a severe knot, face scrubbed, finished with a dab of lip gloss. She looked younger.

"I have to go to the bank, and I have to go this morning," she said.

"Yeah, I could tell you was going out," he answered.

"So, you'll have to take Evan with you this one time. Now be good and promise me you won't go back to the Dead Zone," she said unexpectedly.

"What? Mrs. Garvey, the story! I need it!"

"Please, Jake. It's too dangerous."

"Mrs. Garvey, I'm safer there than on the streets."

"You're probably right," she sighed. "Go on and do what you have to do. I guess it's just the nagging of an old mind, but the storyteller bothers me."

"I'll tell you the rest of the story, I promise."

"I'd rather you didn't. It's begun to make me uneasy. I'm afraid it leaves me with a strange sense of a trailing nightmare."

"Okay, whatever you want," he said, leaning over to kiss her on the cheek as she left.

He washed Evan, pulled a tight cap on his head and sat him in a stroller his ma used to push. Evan was too big for it, but not as much too big as a seven-year-old should have been.

"Come on, Mellie. We're gonna be late."

They took turns pushing Evan. Alvin was standing by the gate house.

"Late as usual. I've been waiting for you. No school today. They called it off so they could re-evaluate what to do next. I think they just want things to cool down."

"No school?" Jake repeated.

"Holiday," Alvin said. "Now who's this little guy?"

"Evan, my brother. He's seven."

"He don't come to school?"

"He's sick," Jake said.

"Plague, huh?" Alvin said. "My little cousin looked like that. Sorry, so sorry."

"Yeah! How come you ain't scared?"

"Aside from the fact I been vaccinated? It's too late to be scared. We shoulda been scared before the Plague hit. Now, it's mainly over, and it's too late," he said again. "Now off you go, so I can go home, too."

"What are we gonna do, Jake?" Mellie asked.

"Go to the Zone."

"With Evan?"

"Sure. We'll tram part way. He's a safety ticket. Mrs. Garvey gave me lunch money for all of us, so we can get tickets instead."

The tram was empty except for a few old ladies who had all dyed their hair pink and had it permed into tight curls. Patting her hair, one of them said, "I tried the dye out on my cat first. Now I got a pink and black cat. She's the talk of my building."

"That'd be something," Mellie whispered to Jake.

"Me, I accidentally dropped dye in my toilet bowl and now when the neighbors downstairs do dishes, their water is bright pink."

"Yuck, Mildred, I'm glad I don't live near you."

"Me, too," Jake whispered back to Mellie.

"Well, my canary got into my dye and now he's all pink," the third lady announced.

"And he probably blows pink bubbles when he sings," Mellie giggled.

The three old ladies turned to stare at them, just as the tram stopped.

"Oh my, this is our stop," Mildred cried out in distress. "Quick, quick, pull the cord, Rosie."

"I can't. My hands are full."

Jake jerked on the cord and the old ladies toddled off, falling into each other, pink heads colliding. Jake and Mellie burst out laughing. Evan opened his eyes, and closed them again.

They finally came to the end of the line, but a long way from where they wanted to be. Jake pushed the stroller as fast as he could until they reached the end of the walk, and the fields of the Zone lay before them. They stashed the stroller in an empty door frame and Jake hoisted Evan onto his back. The little boy's arms hung limply around his neck. Jake sighed. No more hope, Ma, he thought.

They didn't see the storyteller, but climbed to the roof. The wind whistled through their hair and Mellie zipped her jacket.

"It's too cool for the roof today," the storyteller said from the stairwell. "Come," he motioned to them.

They followed him into a back room with soft cushions on the floor and a little, pot-bellied stove that was puffing out heat.

"Is this Evan?" he asked, cocking a pale head at the boy where he lay limply on the pillows.

"Yeah. Mrs. Garvey had an errand and they closed school for the day because of the riot, so we came here."

"Ah," the storyteller said, "and you want more story?" They nodded and he smiled. "Fine, then today we finish it."

They spent many days, that turned to many months, in cold flight, and the child turned a little older and Acob turned twenty-six. She was a beautiful child, and in each month that passed, Acob became more and more determined that he would not leave her on the ship. She was his child. She was the only person he had loved since they had torn him from his parents. He would not allow the masters to separate them.

He rarely saw the masters in those days, so he and Maylis, as he had named her, roamed the ship. They found a new room filled only with volumes of old books. They opened them gently, and peered into their pages. He read them aloud to Maylis and she soon had a favorite. It was the tale of a wandering scribe who went from place to place, seeking the world's best story. His name was Jabor and he had many adventures. As he went he wrote those adventures down, side-by-side with the stories people told, always seeking that elusive tale that would satisfy his lust for the best story in the world.

Finally he came to a small town where a beautiful girl lived. She cared for three younger children to whom she loved to tell stories. Her hair was night-black, her eyes green-glass, her face sun-yellow, and as Jabor sat with her and listened, he saw the colors of the world pass before him. Her stories were wonderful, but he could not decide which was the most wondrous, so he found himself returning to listen to her day after day.

He worried and worried over the question, and because he could not decide, and because she was always telling another story and another, he kept writing them down and kept worrying over the problem.

Soon he had stayed a year and then another, always writing, always worrying. He married the girl, they had a child and another and another, and still the girl, now a woman, wove her yarns.

Now he wrote those yarns and the everyday stories from the town side-by-side, and his book grew to volumes. He grew old and his handwriting grew shakier and one day his wife found him in tears.

'What's the matter, dear Jabor?' she asked, taking his hands in hers.

'I shall never find the perfect story,' he cried.

'Perfect? Why you already have,' she said laughing at him.

'Which one?" he said. 'Which one?'

'Why, it is the one you have been writing all these years.'

'I have written so many down.'

'No, no. Not the ones you recorded, not my little stories. Your story. The whole thing, all woven together, just like life.'

He blinked.

'Here,' she said, 'read it all over. You will see.'

"The Story Collector" was Maylis' favorite. "How many tales do you think he wrote down in his life? One hundred, a thousand, a million? I want to be a writer, too," she exclaimed each time they read it.

It made Acob smile to see her so delighted.

One night he stood at the port where he and Timiial had first held hands. He felt a brief moment of longing. Turning to leave, he found a master standing behind him.

"Come, look from this other portal."

Below him was a blue and green, cloud-covered world. It hung like a marbled jewel in the blackness.

"This is to be your world."

"This? Now?"

"Yes. It is time, but first you must learn of it. Come, it will be important for you to know all you can of this planet."

"Now? Tonight?"

"Of course."

He followed the master numbly. The assembly room was cold and full of empty echoes.

"You, Acob, are hampered by a physical defect," the master began to explain.

"So I have been told," he interrupted bitterly.

"Listen to me and stop being so angry. There is too much for you to learn before you depart to waste the time on anger."

"I'll try."

"We are sorry for the mistake that was made when we took you for Colony, but all we can do now is to prepare you for your new world. We, as a race, age slowly, unless we have shifted to a shorter-lived life form. Since you cannot shift properly, you will have a very long life. You could, of course, shift into an identity that already exists. Unfortunately, this would have the effect of creating two identical beings. You would be drawn to your twin and to his memories. You would be driven to fill his place in life with all the consequences that implies, and, of course, that is anathema to us."

"I know. "

"No matter how lonely you become, remember, you must not be tempted. It is possible that if you were exposed as an imposter, and submitted to medical examination, you could be detected as an alien being. On this world below us, you would most probably become an object of study, instead of a person, for they are both drawn to and fearful of the unknown. Then two lives would have been lost, yours and your twin's."

"The beings on this world do not sound too attractive," Acob commented.

"Perhaps not, but they resemble us closely enough that you should be able to blend in and go relatively unnoticed if you are careful. There is great variety in their appearance, and also many deformities among them, which we hope will add to your protection."

"You mean they may mistake me for a monstrosity?"

"Perhaps. Even so, you should find an isolated place in which to live."

"I'm used to isolation," he nodded.

"And of course, because you are not shifting, you will have to learn their language consciously. Again, their outward physical similarity to our second stage, the stage you are in, will help with this. You will begin your studies of their world and language tomorrow."

"Wait, what of Maylis?"

"We have told you, she will stay will us."

"But, it will not be so long before she can shift. She can hide until then with me."

"No, she is still too young to hold even our second stage

form for long. She will have to stay and you must go. We have been unable to find any other option."

"She is my family. I want to take her with me."

"She is no one's family. She remains on the ship."

"But, you will let her Colonize with you if she is ready in time?"

"We have told you and told you, Acob, we would like to, but we do not have that long on the ship. It is not your fault, nor ours. Her parents doomed her when they had her. How can you not see this?" the master said, turning on his heel.

"What difference if she dies on this cold ship or in my arms?" he asked the departing back, but got no answer.

There was ,of course, no answer. They intended, in the end, to leave Maylis alone on a dying ship. He would not allow it.

The next morning he brought her with him to the lessons.

Evan chose that moment to begin thrashing. The convulsion was fierce and when Jake felt him he was burning with fever.

"We gotta go," he said desperately. "Evan's sick."

"We'll come back to hear the end," Mellie said, helping Jake bundle Evan into a blanket.

When they got to the doorway where they had stashed the stroller, it was gone.

"What are we gonna do, Mellie? We can't carry him the whole way."

"You're gonna take Evan back to the tower, and I'll go call Mrs. Garvey to come here."

"Yeah, okay," Jake agreed shakily.

He kissed Evan again and again and held him tight. "Please don't die, Evan. Not yet," he murmured into the child's ear and then turned to Mellie.

"Be careful, Mellie. Go straight to the nearest phone drop, punch in and come back. Mrs. Garvey will get here.

I saw a drop only three blocks down by that warehouse. Here, take this," he said, handing her his knife. "And this," he said, punching his cap down and tucking her curls into it. "And swagger like a guy, okay?"

"Yeah, yeah, I'll catch up to you."

He hurried back the way they'd come. Clutching Evan, he stumbled into the dusky first floor of the tower. He padded quickly up the stairs, whispering, "Mr. Adam, please, we need your help."

The only answer was the echoing of his words in the stone stairwells. He climbed a flight of stairs. A round window stared out into the empty Zone.

"Cold and empty. Ain't that how Mr. Adam described space in the story? Yeah, Evan, I think it was."

He noticed a door hidden in deep shadows, and on an impulse pushed through it into a room. There were no windows, but light from a fireplace brushed the walls and in the middle of the floor, lay the sleeping storyteller. Unaware of Jake's presence, his eyes were veiled by translucent lids, and his hands lay exposed on his chest, huge and misjointed. Evan moaned in his sleep. The man sat straight up. His eyes snapped open and seemed to float like two glowing balls in the middle of the windowless room.

"It's me and Evan," Jake said quickly. "We couldn't get home. Mellie went to call Mrs. Garvey to meet us here. Sorry, I didn't mean to scare you. Is it okay we came back?"

The man blinked and his eyes didn't seem to glow at all. It must have been a reflection from the fire.

"Of course, Jake. Here, let's put him close to the hearth. Does he like books? Maybe we can read to him?"

"He used to, but I don't know. He's so sick! I don't know if anything matters to him anymore."

"Should Mellie be alone on the streets?" the storyteller asked. "I could go and wait for her."

"HERE TAKE THIS," HE SAID HANDING HER HIS KNIFE. "AND THIS," HE SAID PUSHING HIS CAP DOWN AND TUCKING HER CURLS INTO IT. "AND SWAGGER LIKE" "GUY OKAY"

"YEAH... YEAH. I'LL CATCH UP TO YOU."

HE HURRIED BACK THE WAY THEY'D COME CLUTCHING EVAN. HE STUMBLED INTO THE DUSKY FIRST FLOOR OF THE TOWER. HE PADDED QUICKLY UP THE STAIRS, WHISPERING, "MR. ADAM, PLEASE, WE NEED YOUR HELP."

THE ONLY ANSWER WAS THE WALLS ECHOING HIS WORDS COLDLY BACK AT HIM.

HE CLIMBED A FLIGHT OF STAIRS, A ROUND WINDOW STARED OUT INTO THE EMPTY ZONE.

"COLD AND EMPTY. ISN'T THAT A HOX WAS ADAM DESCRIBED SPACE IN

THE STORY, YEAH... EVAN. I THINK IT WAS."

HE NOTICED A DOOR HIDDEN IN DEEP SHADOWS AND EVAN IN A USER PUSHED THROUGH IT INTO A ROOM. THERE WERE NO WINDOWS, BUT LIGHT FROM A FIREPLACE BRUSHED THE WALLS AND IN THE MIDDLE OF THE FLOOR LAY SLEEPING STORYTELLER UNAWARE OF JAKE'S PRESENCE. HIS EYES WERE VEILED BY TANSLUSCENT LIDS, AND HIS HANDS LAY EXPOSED ON HIS CHEST, HUGE AND MISSHAPED. EVAN MOANED IN HIS SLEEP. THE MAN SAT STRAIGHT UP. HIS EYES SNAPPED OPEN AND SEEMED TO FLOAT LIKE TWO GLOWING BALLS

IN THE MIDDLE OF THE WINDOWLESS ROOM.

"Yeah, that'd be good," Jake nodded. "I didn't like leaving her, but we didn't have no choice."

Alone with Evan, Jake looked around at the books in the room. Covered in bindings of strange textures and design, the edges of the pages glowed warmly. He opened one. The script was nothing he had ever seen, not that he'd seen much. He opened another. The script was the same, but it had pictures. The people were all distorted. What a rotten illustrator.

The next book was normal. He sank into the story, holding the book in one hand and Evan's hot hand in his other. His eyes dropped and he shook his head, feeling too warm and comfortable. He got up, paced and worried, felt his heart thumping too fast. Finally, Mellie pushed through the door, dragging Mrs. Garvey behind her.

"Where's Mr. Adam?" he asked Mellie.

"I don't know. He was here a minute ago."

"Now then, let's get this fever down," Mrs. Garvey said, kneeling by Evan, and holding something to his lips. "This isn't good, I must say."

"Is he gonna make it?" Jake asked, not really wanting an answer.

"Probably. This time, he probably will. By tomorrow we should be able to go home."

"Maybe Mr. Adam will tell us the rest of the story tonight," Mellie said.

"Maybe, if he comes back."

"He doesn't seem to like me," Mrs. Garvey commented. "I can't imagine what I've done to him."

"Maybe he senses you're uneasy around him," Jake suggested gently.

"Perhaps. I hope I haven't offended him. Perhaps we did know each other before, and that's why his presence nags at me. If he comes back, maybe I'll be able to place where I know him from," she mused.

The night passed and Jake watched through the port-hole as the dawn crept up, gray and dreary before Mr. Adam walked in with an arm load of wood. He knelt without saying anything, throwing wood onto the fire, and soon it was toasty in the room.

"I've brought some breakfast along," he said simply.

"Will you finish the story?" Mellie asked eagerly.

His eyes darted to Mrs. Garvey and away again. "I suppose. Perhaps we do have time. It's drizzling, and I think you should wait to leave."

He served them toast and jam and fresh apples. He brewed a mild tea and Jake held some to Evan's lips. They wiped their fingers on wet cloths and settled in to listen.

"Mr. Adam, do we know each other?" Mrs. Garvey asked before he began.

"No, not really. Years ago I watched you from afar," he said quickly. "Admiration, I guess. After all, you are Eloise Garvey, aren't you? Now let me pick up the tale. Where was I? Ah, yes, I remember."

CHAPTER 24

The school room swallowed them into its emptiness.

"What is the child doing here?" the master demanded.

"Does she have any other place she needs to be?" Acob asked. "If not, she is here."

The master shook his head and began again.

"If you want to survive on this world, you must learn its language and its customs, some of which will seem strange. They are always dressed, except when they wash of course."

"Always?" Acob repeated.

"You will pass best as one of their males, though of course they do not have male nodes. They reproduce in an altogether different manner, but this will not affect you."

"Why not?"

"Because you cannot shift, and therefore you will not reproduce on this world."

"Perhaps if you had not been so loathe to talk of reproduction with us, Maylis would not be an orphan."

"She would not even exist," the master pointed out.

Of course the master was right about that. Even so, it would still be one more loss if he could not find a way to take Maylis with him. He focused back on the lesson.

"These beings live in heavily constructed, awkward cities and scatter themselves across most of their land masses, which are extensive. They are frequently violent, as groups and as individuals."

"And these are the people you chose for me to live among?"

"It was the only group that resembles us closely enough for you to have any measure of protection. There are some pleasant aspects to them. They have music and art and write stories. They are great tool makers. In some places they have set aside vast tracks of untouched lands to be cherished."

Acob had become wiser in his years on the ship. He knew that these things could be blessings or curses, and he knew that his choices had given out years before, so he only nodded.

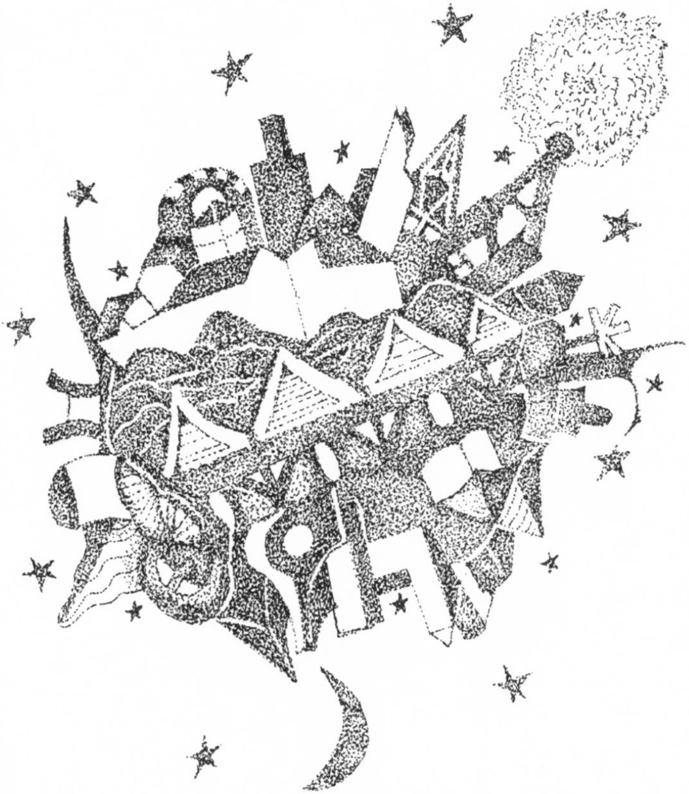

"Sounds like our world," Jake commented.

"Does it?" the storyteller asked and went on.

Acob studied the language and came to be able to read their poetry. He studied their art and came to be able to recognize the works of their painters and sculptors. He listened to their music until he could hum their tunes and Maylis could play them on his flute. And he read their stories until he hoped he understood how they felt and thought, although he could see they had many ways of thinking.

By the time he felt prepared, he also felt sure that if he could take Maylis with him, she could survive until her shifting time would begin. If only he could make the masters relent.

He begged, he pleaded, and finally he plotted.

On the day he turned another year, he was to descend. They had chosen a deserted block of land. He packed his belongings. Then he packed Maylis and took her with him to the port.

They went an hour early, hand-in-hand, and when the masters arrived, they beheld two Maylises, each exactly like the other.

"What is this?" the masters asked, surprise etched on their faces.

"We are Maylis. We are Acob," the two said.

"This is not funny."

The two Maylises did not smile. "No?"

"Acob, stop this."

"No," they answered in unison as they had been practicing.

"Why are you doing this?"

"Is it not obvious?" they answered.

The masters were dismayed. "You would force us to send you both?"

Now the Maylises smiled.

"We cannot," the masters said.

"Then neither of us will go," they said in perfect chorus.

For hours the masters debated, begged, debated some more.

Finally one stepped forward and said, "We will have to send you both. Maylis' death will be on your head now, instead of ours, Acob."

"Death now or later," they answered in tandem.

"What difference? " they said in chorus.

And they were sent.

CHAPTER 25

The storyteller was quiet now.

"Is that it?" Mellie asked.

"No, but I am trying to decide what ending to tell you," the storyteller said.

"Are there different ones?" Jake asked.

"Several, I suppose," he answered.

Jake took a moment to touch Evan. His brother felt like a dry leaf.

"Mrs. Garvey?" he asked.

"Yes, Jake," she said, a heavy book in her hands and a perplexed frown wrinkling her brow.

"Is Evan worse?"

"Oh, Jake, it can only really go that way." She rubbed Evan's head softly. "I wish I could cure him, but I can't."

She opened the book and glanced at it, turning fragile pages that whispered like thin branches brushing each other in the wind. "This is very old," she said.

Jake saw that it was in a foreign script, and asked, "What language is that?"

"One you wouldn't know," the storyteller said.

"But the pictures look familiar," Mrs. Garvey murmured. "Is this 'The Book of the Story Collector'?"

The storyteller looked up, surprise flashing across his pale face. "Yes," he said shakily. "How do you know it?"

"I vaguely remember my older brother reading it to me when I was little," she smiled.

"'The Story Collector'?" Jake asked. "Wasn't that the book Maylis loved?"

"Yes, yes. It was such an easy one to incorporate into the story," the old man answered smoothly.

Jake had an impulse to hold Evan. He gathered him

into his lap, like a small puppy, hot and panting with the fever. He leaned over and kissed the little face.

"Jake," the storyteller said, "I think you four should go home now. Tomorrow or the next day, I can finish."

"Sure, yeah," Jake said. "You're right. Evan needs to go home now."

The trip back was slow until a cabby picked them up. Evan was in a deep sleep, but a bit cooler.

"Mrs. Garvey, why Evan?" he asked, as they tucked him into bed.

"That's a question everyone who loses a child asks. I don't know, Jake. It seems a waste, doesn't it?"

"It's not fair. I guess Ma was right when she said my hope for him was wishful thinking."

"I must have been doing some wishful thinking myself. I was sure he enjoyed my books," Mrs. Garvey said.

"Yeah? Maybe I'll read to him tonight anyways. Whatcha think?"

Mrs. Garvey hugged him. Jake went to the library to choose a book, his eyes running along the shelves and stacks. At the top was a silvery binding which looked familiar. Pulling it down, it nearly clunked him in the head and fell open into his arms. It was a copy of *The Story Collector*, also in the strange script.

"Hey, Mrs. Garvey, can you read this?" he called.

"That?" she asked. "No, you know I can't."

"Then why you got a copy?"

She shook her head as if trying to clear it. "I must have found it on the street. I'm to bed," she answered unsteadily. "But, first, you do know, Jake, that Evan is close to the end?"

He nodded.

"There's more. Because he has the Plague, no one will bury him after it's over."

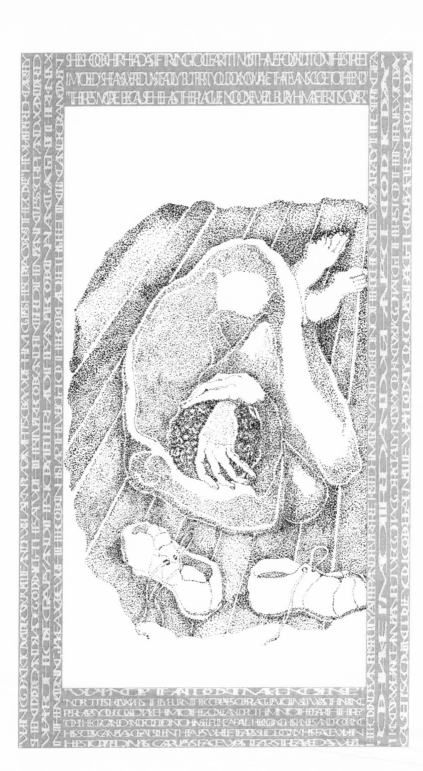

"Why not? That don't make no sense."

"No, but it's how it is. They burn the corpses of Plague victims. I was thinking, perhaps you could take him to the Zone and put him into the earth there?"

"Oh," he groaned and folded himself into a ball, hugging his knees and rocking. His sobs came as great, silent heaves while tears slid down his face. When he stopped, Mrs. Garvey's face was tear streaked as well.

"When I go back tomorrow, Mellie and I will ask Mr. Adam if it's okay with him. I guess he sorta owns the Zone," he whispered hoarsely.

She nodded and said goodnight. He sat with the silver book, fingering the meaningless script, and wondered why both Eloise Garvey and the storyteller had the same book in a language neither knew.

In the morning, Jake awoke with the book in his lap. The weight of it had left his feet tingling and for a moment he thought that he had held Evan all night. Touching the hard corners of the book brought him fully awake. He shook his head and pushed slowly to his feet, which were awakening from full numbness. He found Evan blissfully asleep and fever-free, kissed him gently and ducked into the kitchen. Mellie was already there, sipping tea.

"Oh, Jake, I'm so tired, and we got school today."

"I know watcha mean, but we gotta go and I gotta get the rest of the interview today, too, cause it's coming due. You look beat, Mellie. Why don't you come straight home after school today."

"No way I'm gonna miss the end of the story! No way you leave me behind, Jake Lawrence," she snapped.

"Okay, okay, come. I'm sorry," he said.

"Mrs. Garvey told me Evan's in the wait stage. She said it might last two days or so, and then ..." Tears ran down her cheeks.

"Yeah, I know," he said, hugging her and remembering the other thing he had to ask Mr. Adam. "Come on." He wiped her tears with his finger. "School time don't wait for us, only Alvin does."

She smiled and went to get dressed. When they reached the gates kids were lined up, waiting.

"Hey, Jake, Mellie," Arty greeted them. "The gate's still locked. Alvin ain't here and the school looks empty. Mr. Ap-pel is up at the front using the Gate Keeper's phone. He was told we had school today. Mrs. Percy's up there too, but it don't look good."

"They'll open," Jake said. "They don't want no more riots."

"Hope you're right," someone else said.

Jake took Mellie's hand and pushed to the fore.

"Hey, Mr. Ap-pel, any luck?" Jake called.

"Not yet."

Jake scratched his head. All the teachers were standing by looking lost and uneasy.

"You all thought we was gonna have school?" he asked Mrs. Percy.

She nodded back.

"Well, why don't you just open the gate, and go in, and have school?"

"A good idea, Jake, except none of us know how to open the gates, and Alvin is missing."

Jake grinned. Mellie grinned. Marvin Jones grinned. The smile spread through the crowd of kids. Jake stepped up to the box.

"You know, Mr. Ap-pel, when you're a Streetie kid and you're late as much as me, you kinda, well, figure it out, just in case, you know."

He reached past the teacher and punched in a complex series of beeps and rings, combinations of letters, numbers, and symbols, and the gates rolled open.

"Hadda protect myself from being locked out some day," he smiled at the teachers' dismayed faces. "Now, to classes. You teachers better hurry or us kids are gonna beat you there. I'll lock it up behind everybody."

As he closed the gates behind the chattering crowd, he heard an alarm go off in the Gate Keeper's control array. Someone would come check now. Maybe the array would even be able to say who had opened the gate from his thumb prints. Could be the computer main frame already knew. He hoped Alvin was okay. He went to class.

He was in Mrs. Percy's class when the Gizmo officials arrived. Mrs. Percy raised her white-haired head and said with dignity, "May I help you, gentlemen?"

"We're looking for someone."

"Oh, is that so? And why is that?" she asked.

"I'm sure you can figure that out."

"Yes, I can," she answered. "You're upset because we are having classes."

"We had determined it would be unwise to hold classes in this school."

"And why was that, gentlemen? As you can see, we are peacefully in the midst of learning. Everyone is working. Nothing has been amiss all day, except for the fact that you tried to lock us out."

"And that brings us to whom we are looking for. It is a particular student. Jake Lawrence."

Jake sighed, and was about to stand when Marvin said, "That's me."

"Aw, shut it up, it ain't you," Mikel said, "it's me."

"No you don't, you guys. I'm him," George joined in.

Jake stood. "Thanks, guys, but it's okay. I'm Jake."

"Hey," Petey Jarall called out. "You creep, it was me what opened the gate. I'm Jake."

It was just like the shape shifters' trick in their class, only without the shifting. A lot more kids chimed in, claiming to be Jake.

"Stop this," the Gizmos yelled. "Mrs. Percy, which student is he?"

"Gentlemen, this class is studying deductive reasoning. Go deduce!"

The kids all laughed. Jake held his breath.

"Fine, hold your class for now. It won't help. There is no hope here, not for any of you now!"

"Oh really?" Mrs. Percy asked. "I'd say, that as of today, there is a lot more hope for these children than there ever has been."

The Gizmos stomped out muttering and angry, but they left. The door closed and Mrs. Percy kept on teaching as if nothing had happened. Five minutes before the period was over she stopped teaching, smiled broadly and said quietly, "Congratulations, you were stupendous!"

At lunch the cafeteria was abuzz with chatter, when in walked the same Gizmos.

"Jake Lawrence, please step forward. Within a few moments we'll have your thumbprint ID anyway, so do yourself and everyone a favor and step forward now."

No one moved. Finally Mellie stood and said, "Whatcha want him for? He ain't done nothing."

"That isn't for you to determine, young lady."

"Right? Well, what I wanna know is, who gave you guys the right to lock us out? The rule has always been, if you showed up on time, you could go to school."

"School is a place to learn. How can anyone learn here?" one Gizmo asked, gesturing at the shabby walls.

Now Jake stood. "We do, that's all. Ask us something. Ask us where we learned the meaning of persuasive argument?"

"Oh, for heaven's sake!"

"Or genetic probability?"

"Kids' stuff," another Gizmo declared.

"Yeah? Well, maybe, but ain't we kids, so learning kid stuff should be about right," Jake replied.

"And I might add," Mr. Ap-pel said from a doorway, "apt ones. What do your own children study, sirs?"

"Computer language," one of them said.

"Ours study Shakespeare's language, and if they stay long enough, Faulkner, Longfellow, Borges, Homer and Boorstin. Do your children study these as well?"

"Of course not. That was outdated before the end of the twentieth. They study micro-chip engineering and the technology of mass psychology."

"Why, sir? So they can make more gizmos and use them for some valuable purpose? Like to make mankind wealthier? We're mankind, right here. What kind of wealth do you offer us, do your children plan for us?"

"This is ridiculous! You people are ungrateful."

"No sir," Mr. Ap-pel countered. "We are very grateful for this school. That is exactly the point. We are grateful and wish to remain here. We are not a threat to you. We don't study what you do. We will probably never be materially wealthy. Leave us here. What harm can it do?"

A Gizmo, who had said nothing until then, spoke softly. "I see you are very persuasive, Mr. Appel. For the moment you have won the day. Ladies and gentlemen," the man said, turning to the kids, "you have just been treated to a magnificient demonstration by a master of persuasive argument."

The Gizmo began to applaud.

The kids joined in, slowly, then more loudly and with an even louder crescendo as the Gizmos slipped out the door.

CHAPTER 26

"That was something," Mellie said as they made their way to the Zone after school.

"Yeah, Mr. Ap-pel was stupendous!"

"So were you, Jake."

She punched him in the arm, then took his hand. Suddenly she pulled him to her and kissed him, really softly on the lips. They broke clean and walked on, swinging their arms, joined at the hands.

"I wonder what the rest of Mr. Adam's story is." Jake murmured when they reached the Zone.

The sun-yellow blooms next to the tower had been joined by lemon-tinged ones that gently rested their heads on the charred stone. The dusk birds sang their throaty song a bit early in the fading afternoon sun, reaching into the stairwells of the tower in an echoing call. Somewhere a peeping chorus joined them.

"What's that?" Mellie asked.

"Spring Peepers," the storyteller said, greeting them. "A tiny bit of a frog, the length of your thumb, makes all that noise."

"Wow," Jake said, "what a noise from such a little fellow!"

"Lots of little ones at once. Are they not beautiful trillers?" the old man asked.

"Yeah," Jake agreed.

The evening was balmy as they settled on the roof. A breeze fingered their cheeks as the last chapter unfolded.

They landed with two volumes of 'The Story Collector' and a few other books, Acob's flute and childhood possessions, and nothing more. Their landing field was full of trees and grasses, but the people of this world considered it empty because it had no buildings. Maylis and Acob wandered about until darkness began

to descend and they realized they needed shelter. They spent the first evening huddled against each other while Acob worried over the wisdom of bringing a child along. They were used to the even temperatures of the ship. Here it vacillated within an hour from pleasant to shivering. The evening seemed endless, but at last the yellow sun rose into the lightening, blue sky.

"It is beautiful," Maylis said.

Yes, Acob thought.

They spent the first day wandering, dreading the coming night. Despairing of shelter, Acob thought of entering a city, but looking at Maylis, knew that even if he could pass for human, she could not.

"It's Earth they came to?" Jake asked.

Mr. Adam nodded.

"What did Maylis look like?" Mellie asked.

"Not quite formed. Her hands were still webbed at the second knuckle joint, her eyes not completely cleared to a single color, her skin so translucent you could see her organs. Her head was large and she was thin. She had at least another year to go before she would maybe be able to pass for human, and more before she could shift."

"Boy, you sure get specific with this story," Mellie said, shaking her head in clear amazement.

Real specific, Jake thought, maybe too specific.

"I have had lots of time to imagine it in lots of detail. Shall I go on with the story?" Mr. Adam asked.

"Sure, but first, what's the 'J' stand for in your name?" Jake asked.

"I've been waiting for you to ask that. It stands for Jacob," the man said, but almost pronounced it without the J, almost like Acob. Jake saw Mellie glance his way and he shrugged ever so slightly.

She was so innocent, so small. We stumbled about for several days, drawn ever nearer to the edge of the city. On the fourth day we stumbled onto this very tower. The inside was in tatters, but it offered us shelter. We crawled into it and collapsed. Mice crawled over us, coons played on the stairs as we huddled in terror. Remember, we had never seen such animals. I suppose we would have been laughed at by your classmates. Sometimes I wish I could smile as humans do. It's one of your loveliest traits.

The storyteller had switched person deliberately, calmly staring them in the eyes.

"Do you want me to go on?"

Jake looked back at him. "Sure," he said, "but why switch your story now?"

"I trust you. Do you want me to go on?"

Jake took a deep breath. An unease was dawning in him. He remembered the book in Mrs. Garvey's apartment. "Yeah, go on. It's too late to turn back now, ain't it?"

"Did Maylis survive?" Mellie asked.

"Oh yeah, she did, didn't she?" Jake said.

"Yes, Jake, she did."

She reached shifting age and I tutored her, just as the masters had tutored us. She was a naturally quick study. She studied the people who sometimes wandered into our presence. And she studied the magazines and books I pilfered for her. I was amazed the first time I ventured among you. Everyone ignored me. They pretended I looked just like them! The masters had chosen well for me. I got much information for her without much danger to us.

At last she was ready to shift, and yet she hesitated.

"What will happen to you when I go?" she asked.

"Nothing. I will go on."

"Alone?" she asked.

"As it must be."

"It isn't fair," she said.

Of course she was right, but there was nothing I could do except quote you humans, "Life isn't fair."

Finally she told me she had chosen a shift form. She had an image in her mind that satisfied her, but that before she shifted she would tell me her new name, so that when I was lonely I could send a message and she would come to me.

I never told her she wouldn't remember me.

"Oh," Mellie said, "that is so sad. Do you know what became of her?"

"He does," Jake answered. "Let's go home now."

"What happened to her?" Mellie insisted. "I wanna know."

"No, Mellie," Jake said. "Come on, I gotta check on Evan."

"Why won't you let him answer, Jake?"

"Cause it's none of our business. Now come on. It's late. The scavengers and gangs are gonna be out already. The sooner we go, the better."

"Say hello to Mrs. Garvey for me," Acob Dam called.

"We will," Jake said.

"Yes, good-bye," the man called.

CHAPTER 27

Jake hurried Mellie along. It was balmy enough that the streets were packed. Walkers peddled their bodies, swishing and preening for buyers. Petty thieves brazenly sold their wares, knowing this was their time and they had nothing to fear. A gang of Tattoos sauntered around a corner, and Mellie and Jake ducked into a shadowy door frame, holding their breath until the multi-colored beasts had passed. The tram stops were jammed with Tattoos who hooted and strutted, kings of the hill in the wee hours. Jake and Mellie walked past them, leaning their heads face-to-face like lovers, hiding their identities from the patterned faces.

Jake had always felt at home in the streets, but now he felt removed, as if an alien seeing humanity for the first time. Acob Dam must have been amazed when he passed through unnoted, but then who in this throng could point a finger at another's deformity.

It was almost midnight before they tumbled into bed, but within a few moments Mrs. Garvey was shaking him.

"Jake, it's Evan. He's in the last stage."

"No! How long before ...?"

"Probably a few hours."

He followed her into Evan's room. His eyes were open, and foam was bubbling with a little spitting sound on his lips.

"You should take him soon to the Zone. Did you ask Mr. Adam about burying him there?"

"I forgot," he mumbled. "Get him ready for me," he said, rubbing tears away from his eyes. "I'll take him. Don't wake Mellie. I don't want her to know."

"Here, take this money for a cabby. Remember, school is only five or six hours away."

"I'll try to get back. Oh yeah, Mr. Adam said 'Hi'."

"That was nice," she said absently. She kissed Evan. "Oh, sweet child, I am so sorry. I am going to miss you, oh yes, I am going to."

Jake pulled a hood over Evan's face so the cabby wouldn't see him. Evan looked so small now, the cabby would think he was younger and needed to be carried.

The ride was slow through the night streets. Jake's mind whirled around his brother. Evan as a new born, tiny fists flailing, eyes wide with wonder. Evan with his first fever, the first glazed look. Evan! If only his brother could shift, become another person, but he was only a human. In a short while, Jake would have no one, no one, just like Acob.

"No one" spun in his mind as he paid the cabby and stepped into the Zone. It wasn't fair that he was losing Evan. It wasn't fair that Acob had lost Maylis either. At least Maylis had lived, but she had still been lost to Acob. Slowly Jake's mind twisted around everything, in and out, back and forth. Suddenly his steps picked up. He began to run, praying, "Evan, not yet, not yet. Wait a bit."

"Acob," he screamed into the tower. "Acob Dam, come quick, now!"

He saw a thin line of light travel down the stairs and coalesce into Acob Dam.

"He's dying right now," Jake sobbed breathlessly.

"I am so sorry, Jake."

"Yeah, me too," he said, tears streaming down his face, "but don't you see? It's your chance!"

"Chance? For what?"

"To shift, Mr. Adam. To shift. To be Evan."

"What?"

"It's not just your chance. It's mine, too, and Evan's! It's my chance to have a real, whole brother, for Evan to be a real person, not just a dry shell. And it's your chance to be with Mrs. Garvey again! You can be together. She already loves Evan. She can love you again. Please, don't let my brother die completely. Please!"

"I don't know, Jake. I have to think about it."

"No, you can't. It'll be too late. He's dying right now. Shift, please, take him and shift while there's time."

Acob Dam took the little boy in his arms. "You understand, I won't really be Evan?" he asked Jake.

"I know, but you'll grow and play and learn, and in a way you'll be Evan. And in any case, you'll be my brother, cause I'll love you and teach you, like you loved and taught Maylis."

"And what will Mrs. Garvey say? What will you tell her?"

"I guess I'll tell her it was a miracle and she'll hafta believe cause how else could she explain it. By the way, she don't remember Maylis or Acob, but she vaguely remembers having a brother."

Acob moaned, then looked up. "Remember, Jake Lawrence, I will only recollect being Acob Dam for a short while after the shift, and in that time you must help me as the masters would have, because otherwise the transition is confusing and can be dangerous to the new being."

"Okay, sure. Tell me what I hafta do."

"You must talk to me. Tell me everything you can about what Evan was like. Keep talking. I can only hope that I do not shift into his sick form. I will try to focus on a whole Evan. So, what you tell me will be even more important, for even after the shift, the new being is flexible, will still be changing."

"You gonna remember my telling you these things?"

"No, but I will engrain them, imprint them. It is very, very important."

"The thing is, Evan ain't never been well, so I ain't sure what he woulda been like."

"Then tell me what you wished for him to be like."

"My wishes? I only wished for him to talk, and play, and grow. I wanted him to have fun, and to laugh at funny things, and to be able to learn. That enough?"

"Too general. You must tell him/me specifics. Choose things he would have liked to do if he had been normal. Choose personality traits. Tell him/me about his/my family. Think about it while I take him."

"How long will it take?"

"I do not know exactly, but I think I must hurry before it's too late." He hesitated. "Jake, I have been so lonely, you know."

"Yeah, I know. Me too."

Acob Dam took the limp child up the tower steps.

Two hours later Evan walked down the same steps.

"Come here, Evan," Jake said gently. "Come on, let's go look at the yellow flowers in the sun outside, and the birds, and the trees. Then we'll read together. I know how much you love to read, and learn, and gather information. And let's pretend and imagine a few games and then I'll make some jokes for you to laugh at. We'll find your flute to play, too."

Evan nodded and followed smiling, and when he played the flute the music was a high, clear, complicated song Jake had never heard. Jake told him of a girl named Timiial, of another girl named Maylis, and of bugs on warm window panes. He made Evan read some of *The Story Collector* and translate it as he went.

"Always, always make up stories to tell people and music to play on your flute," Jake told him. "Promise me."

The boy nodded and then picked up the flute again and played wistfully. When he put it down, Evan spoke, "And I will read you the rest of 'The Story Collector', and other books that are here, too."

"We'll come here a lot, I promise, Evan," Jake said.

"And I'll play my music for you and Mellie, and Mrs. Garvey, of course," Evan promised, which reminded Jake to tell him all he knew of Mrs. Garvey, and Mellie, and school and even Alvin, as well.

"Thanks for letting me be your brother," Evan said. His eyes rolled into his head and glazed over for a moment. His body stilled and seemed to become more solid. It was over and complete.

Jake went back up into the tower, gently gathered the wispy body of his brother in his arms, and brought it down to bury it among the yellow bulbs.

"I like yellow," Evan said. "Are there any yellow bugs in our garden?"

"Naw, Evan, no yellow ones."

They walked home in the breaking dawn. Mrs. Garvey was on the front stoop. Evan hid behind Jake as they walked up.

"Oh Jake, I am so very sorry. How are you?" she asked from a puffy, tear-streaked face.

"I'm fine, Mrs. Garvey. Look!" Jake cried, laughing and thrusting Evan into her arms.

"Evan? Oh! Oh! Evan? How?" she cried out.

"I suppose I just wished hard enough, after all!"

Mrs. Garvey looked from Jake to Evan and back again. Then she shut her open mouth and pushed them inside, into the apartment.

"Mellie," she screamed. "Come here, Mellie, quick!"

"Evan?" Mellie whispered. She hugged the little boy and kissed Jake. "How'd you do it?"

"It was a miracle, I guess. I just kept on wishing."

"A miracle?" Mellie asked, cocking her head and walking around Evan.

Mrs. Garvey also cocked her head, running her hands down the child. "Jake, this just isn't possible."

"But here he is, Mrs. Garvey."

"Jake?" she said, not satisfied, demanding more.

"We gotta hurry now. Come on, Mellie," Jake said, cutting off his conversation with Mrs. Garvey. "Let me clean up quick, and we'll walk to school."

"Evan?" Mellie said again, as the little boy smiled and picked up *The Story Collector*, touching its delicate pages gently. He opened the book and began to read it silently.

Mellie bent over the book. "Where'd you get this from, Mrs. Garvey?" she asked as Mrs. Garvey looked up.

"Jake asked me that before," Mrs. Garvey said. "I just remembered, it belonged to my brother."

"Your brother? What was his name?"

Mrs. Garvey scratched her head. "I hadn't thought of him in such a long time. He was lost to me so long, long ago."

"Mrs. Garvey, you got any yellow bugs on your windows?" Evan asked suddenly, pressing his nose against the glass.

"Why, Evan, you can speak! Jake, what on earth? Surely this is more than wishful thinking!" the old lady declared.

Jake shrugged. "It's the only explanation I got. Let's go, Mellie. Maybe in a few days, Evan can start school."

Evan climbed into Mrs. Garvey's lap and kissed her. "This feels so right," Jake heard her say softly.

Just as Mellie and he got to the door, Mrs. Garvey called out, "My brother's name was Jacob, Mellie."

Mellie said almost nothing on the way to school. Alvin was back.

"Hey, Jake, heard you saved the day."

"Naw, it was really Mrs. Percy and Mr. Ap-pel. They're great teachers. Glad you're back, Alvin."

"Me, too! Now hurry, you're late."

"Jake," Mellie said at last, "how's the storyteller?"

"He's gone, Mellie, for good."

"Where'd he go?"

"Oh, you know."

"Yes, I think I do, Jake."

She smiled and took his hand.

See, Ma, wishful thinking! You were wrong, sometimes wishes do come true, Ma. Sometimes, if you're really, really lucky.

A floating spot of yellow and black landed on the pavement, fluttering its flat, scalloped wings against each other.

"Mellie, what's that?" he asked.

"I ain't sure," she said, squatting to stare closely at it.

"It's a butterfly," Mr. Ap-pel said as he walked past. "It's been years since I've seen one."

"Yeah? Is that some kinda bug, Mr. Ap-pel?" Jake asked.

"An insect? Of course," he said.

"Good! I can tell Evan there's some yellow bugs here after all," Jake smiled.

ABOUT THE AUTHOR

Fascinated with the imaginative power of science fiction since she was ten years old, this is Sallie Lowenstein's first published science fiction novel. She says that to start writing science fiction, she first asks "what if" such and such were the case. That inevitably leads her to begin developing another world in great detail, for in order to write this genre, it must be consistent and convincing because it is basically only in existence in the mind. Ms. Lowenstein has been a professional fine artist (painter and stone sculptor) since she was fifteen when she began selling her work. She believes in illustrating all her books, even her novels, and visualizes the art work as she writes the story. Recently she has become interested in the art of hand-made books, and has added the folded book and screens as formats for her two-dimensional fine art.

Ms. Lowenstein lives in the Washington, D.C. metropolitan area with her husband and two teenage children.

If you would like to contact her with questions or comments about her books, to find out how to order a book, or to arrange a personal appearance, you can send her an e-mail at:

lionstone@juno.com

SPECIAL THANKS TO:

Robert, John and Rachel Kenney for their constant support
and many insightful contributions to this book;

M.A. Harper and Frank Louis Lowenstein, whose
comments are always prized;

Kathy Kaplan, Gloria Levine, Susie Loutoo,and Frank and Sheila
Lowenstein, who variously encouraged and supported the author
in the publication of this book;

and
Peggy Irvine of Kirby Lithographic Company, whose patience and
advice on the technical aspects of printing this book were invaluable.